Praise for *Doting*

"The comedy is double-edged, for really no one can know anybody . . ."—*Nation*

"Gleaming new satire . . . in the manner of Green's contemporary Ivy Compton-Burnett. . . . If you are interested in the new modes and experiments in fiction, you'll not want to miss it."—*San Francisco Chronicle*

"The style, made up wholly of dialogue, seems to be round in much the manner of a dog chasing his tail . . . having a hypnotic fascination for the reader."
—*Library Journal*

"Henry Green possesses what Meredith once called the 'comic spirit.' It denotes a humanism, a sense of proportion that is both disinterested and warmly sympathetic."—*New York Times*

"A skillful intaglio of inconstancy which is pleasantly deft and devious."—*Kirkus*

"Continuously enchanting."—*Bookmark*

"Nobody writes novels quite like Henry Green. . . . His characters . . . dance to a tune of his own as precise and stylized as a sonata."—*New York Herald Tribune*

"Witty, stylish, poignant, mordantly funny and horribly sad."—*New Statesman*

BOOKS BY HENRY GREEN

DOTING

HENRY GREEN

Dalkey Archive Press

First Dalkey Archive edition, 2001

Library of Congress Cataloging-in-Publication Data

Green, Henry, 1905-1974.
    Doting / by Henry Green.-- 1st Dalkey Archive ed.
    p. cm.
    ISBN 1-56478-266-2 (alk. paper)
    1. Middle aged men--Fiction. 2. Young women--Fiction. 3.
Friendship--Fiction.   I. Title.
    PR6013.R416 D6 2001
    823'.912--dc21
                                        2001028038

Partially funded by grants from the National Endowment for the Arts, a federal agency and the Illinois Arts Council, a state agency.

Dalkey Archive Press
www.dalkeyarchive.com

NATIONAL
ENDOWMENT
FOR THE ARTS

"Pretty squalid play all round, I thought!"

His son only grunted back at him, face vacant, mouth half open, in London, in 1949.

Smiling with grace the mother, the spouse, leant across to the fourth of their after-the-theatre party, who was a girl older than this boy, aged almost seventeen, by perhaps two years.

"But could you conceive of the wife?" Mrs Middleton cried.

The girl, the Annabel Paynton, smiled.

"Oh wasn't she!" this child agreed who, as a favoured daughter of a now disliked old friend, was invariably asked to make even numbers at what had come to be the immemorial evening out, on the boy's first night of his holidays.

So they were three in full evening dress apart from Peter's tailored pin stripe suit in which, several weeks later, he was to carry a white goose under one arm, its dead beak almost trailing the platform, to catch the last train back to yet another term.

"Pretty fair rot to my ideas" Arthur Middleton insisted, 'rot' being a word he did not use except in his son's holidays. But he had no answer save a long roll of drums, because, at this moment, lights throughout the restaurant were dimmed.

"Not quite ideal for eating" Diana Middleton complained.

"Here, I am truly sorry" the husband apologised, then switched their lamp on to cast violet from the shade upon their table, at which the girl's sweet features turned to no less than wild mystery in the sort of dark he'd made. Perhaps she was aware of this, for she laughed full at Peter until, at last, the boy squirmed.

"And have you been here ever before?" she demanded.

3

"What, at his age!" Mrs Middleton cried.

"Well in that case he's managed it at last" the husband commented as he watched Miss Paynton's face, her eyes. Then, to yet another roll of drums, violet limes were switched on the small stage, a man hurrahed, and Annabel bellied the corsage of her low dress the better to see between elegant shod toes, the party being seated to supper up on a balcony at this night club and hard against wrought iron railings, – she did this the better to watch what now emerged, an almost entirely naked woman who walked on to scant applause, and who carried with some awkwardness, within two arms thin like snakes, a simple wicker, purple, washing basket.

"Well but just look at that" the father said and turned his gaze back to Miss Paynton, while the son opened his mouth as if he could eat what he now saw.

"Now, who's being stuffy dear, please?" Diana asked.

Peter shushed both as, following the drums, a dirge of indigo music rose then sank, or rose, to a single flute with repeated, but ever changing, runs or trills.

"Would you call her pretty, Peter?" the mother asked in a bright voice.

"Fairly awful" he replied. At which Mrs Middleton smiled her fondest.

"All right by me" his father said to Annabel to be snubbed by yet another "sh'sh" from Peter.

For the lady had begun to dance.

All she wore was a blue sequin on the point of each breast and a few more to cover her sex. As she swayed those hips, sequins caught the light to strike off in a blaze of royal blue while the skin stayed moon-lit and the palms of her two hands, daubed probably with a darker pigment, made a deeper shadow above raised arms, of a red so harsh it was almost black in that space through which she waved her opened fingers in figure of eights before the cut jet of two staring eyes.

Mr Middleton did not seem able to leave Miss Paynton be.

"How old would you say she was?" he demanded of the girl in what sounded a salacious whisper. "Every bit of sixteen?"

"Heavens no! Twenty three at least" the young lady answered, in a matter of fact voice, as she continued to watch.

"Come now" he said, louder, and appeared confident. "Any girl with a figure like that could only be a child!"

"Yes, I suppose" Miss Paynton seemed to agree, yet obviously doubted, and flicked him a look.

"Sh . . . Arthur" his wife implored.

"Sorry of course" he answered in a kind of stage whisper upon which, to another, shorter, roll of drums, the spectacle changed, those lights turned to a pink which flushed Annabel's forehead to rose while the woman below stood still, and seemed to swell as saxophones took over to welcome heads of what, it soon became plain, were mechanically operated snakes thrust forth on springs from the now apricot coloured washing basket, and which did not sway their blunt heads, but kept quite quiet to a sudden return of flutes.

"Perpetrated a bit of a bloomer, surely, when they turned their lights full on as she staggered in with the old property basket?" Mr Middleton suggested.

He had no answer. Now, to a crescendo, in which the whole band joined, the woman began to waggle with extreme violence and the limes went red till she seemed almost about to melt in flames beneath.

"Oh God when are we to get something to drink?" Peter protested and turned his face away, frowning.

"I know old chap" Mr Middleton agreed.

"A pint of shandy!" the son wailed.

"And here's poor Annabel been without a drop the whole evening" Diana reminded everyone.

"All in this place's own good time" her husband explained, leaning forward as if he had only now begun to appreciate the good flesh, slopping to music, close below.

"But really, Arthur" his wife grumbled.

"It's all a part of life" he said, without looking back. "They're Sicilians, each one" he said, eyes fixed. "There's not a waiter here will stir before this is over. To them it's a kind of bonus."

"Could I have a cigarette then, d'you think?" the son demanded, almost as a right it seemed, and Diana at once began to rummage in her bag.

"Steady on" his father moaned, but no one paid the least attention.

And Annabel, who had been lending a sort of tolerant amusement to the dance, turned to the boy and said,

"Then you do already, is that it?"

Peter did not trouble to reply.

His father started to watch Annabel again.

"Strange how much nearer in age you two are, both of you, than to Diana or me" he said, looking for a moment, as if in self pity, at his wife who chose to ignore this; thence back once more on Annabel, the Paynton, who was growing yet but was full grown already, lush.

Mrs Middleton having tossed her son a cigarette, passed him her lighter.

"Why not smoke occasionally?" Peter asked the girl. "What's wrong?"

"Plenty of time yet, thanks."

"If you go on saying that, you never will."

His father interrupted. "Yes, my dear, have you ever considered" he said to his wife "only two years between him and any girl who's 'out'?"

"Of course" she replied with a fond smile at Peter. Upon which the act beneath they'd ceased to watch, came to a close in thin applause.

"And then can't you even drink?" Peter asked the girl.

"But I don't want."

"I remember when you used."

"You'd better not" she said, and smiled.

"Now we must and shall get down to serious business" Mr Middleton exclaimed, it can only have been to draw attention to himself again. Rising forty five, on the way to stoutness, he added "I starve for food after a theatre."

His wife put on a loving, superior smile. "If you were just not so greedy you wouldn't gain all this weight" she said "all the time."

In reply he winked at Annabel, an act which Peter did not miss.

"I needn't bother, not at my age" he boasted.

"You don't!" the girl exclaimed. "You can say that and mean it?"

"Now Annabel!" he cried, delightedly laughing. "You shan't make out I ought to bant. My life's half over!"

"Well I do eat anything and it won't upset my stomach" she boasted.

"Mine's like an ostrich, too" he claimed.

"Poor dear, it's his liver" Mrs Middleton told them.

"Thanks darling" her husband said.

"The doctor keeps on repeating he must slim down for his own sake" Mrs Middleton insisted, with a worried frown.

"Now really, my dear we needn't go over all my ailments, not so much in public."

"You know what Dr Adams said, Arthur!"

"Well, where is our waiter? Anyway these young people don't have to consider the size of their meals."

"I could eat a whole steak" Peter announced. "Was that real food they had at the play, d'you suppose?"

"The whisky's forever cold tea" his father told him over a shoulder as he pushed the bell again.

"No honestly, Arthur" Mrs Middleton appealed. "Not whisky, remember! Dr Adams specially warned us."

"Now dear, couldn't you be making me a trifle ridiculous before the children?"

"We aren't children" his son objected, in a bored voice.

There was another roll of drums.

"Why, we're going to have something else" Miss Paynton exclaimed, leaning forward again. Once more the elder Middleton looked down her dress, but, this time, his son caught him at it. And Annabel herself glanced sideways up, to pin the older man down. Upon which the father looked guiltily away, lights were dimmed, so he chanced a quick return to the girl's eyes and, in this half dark, it seemed she steadily regarded him.

"Hard to see down there from here" he remarked to Diana, his wife.

"Is that so?" Annabel sweetly enquired. "Then why don't you lean under the rail like I'm doing?"

Mr Middleton must have blushed, for, in the half light, his face seemed to go black, just as a juggler walked on the small stage.

The man started with three billiard balls. He flung one up and caught it. He flung it up again then sent a second ball to chase the first. In no time he had three, fountaining from out his hands. And he did not stop at that. He introduced, he insinuated one at a time, one more after another, and threw the exact inches higher each time to give six, seven balls room until, to no applause, he had a dozen chasing themselves up then down into his two lazy-seeming hands, each ball so precisely placed that it could be thought to follow grooves in violet air.

"Well surely our Sicilians will find nothing to admire in this" Mr Middleton said, and pushed the bell once more.

A waiter, with little English, came at once and when Diana could not read the bill of fare in this dark, her husband had to raise his lighter like a torch, which caused a commotion because the lady was afeared for her great eyelashes. Chattering away, having fun with the Sicilian who, on being asked how their lobster would be cooked, said 'in rice very nice, in the shell very well' they altogether ignored, as they decided against this lobster, miracles of skill spun out a few feet beneath: – no less than the balancing of a billiard ivory ball on the juggler's chin, then a pint beer mug on top of that ball at the exact angle needed to cheat gravity, and at last the second ivory sphere which this man placed from a stick, or cue, to top all on the mug's handle: – the ball supporting a pint pot, then the pint pot a second ball until, unnoticed by our party, the man removed his chin and these separate objects fell, balls of ivory each to a hand, and the jug to a toe of his patent leather shoe where he let it hang and shine to a faint look of surprise, the artist.

8

But in spite of all this and another roll of drums Miss Paynton insisted on asking Peter,

"D'you know Terence Shone at your place?"

"Who?" he said. "No one of that name!"

"He is there" Annabel assured the boy.

"Well yes, there is a Shone" Peter admitted. "But he's Captain of Games."

"The very one!"

"Not our Prefect" the boy muttered. "Why, how on earth?"

"Oh he's always asking me down."

"What's he like then, Ann?"

"All right."

When the girl said this Mrs Middleton allowed her eyes to come, as though casually, to rest on Annabel's guileless features, where they stayed, with her own great eyelashes batting every now and then like slow, purple butterflies.

"Oh Terry's all of a piece, I suppose" Miss Paynton continued. "Gives me tea in that sort of a club they have."

"The Prefects' Lodgings!!" he cried out. "So what's it like there?"

"So so" she assured him.

"I've never seen you about" he objected.

"Well then, you can't have looked while I've been having tea, that must be it" she replied, and sent a short, sweet smile towards his mother.

"You could introduce them" Mrs Middleton suggested.

"Oh really Mother, would you please mind not being so insane!"

"I know Peter, I know" she apologised. "Arthur, were you as difficult at his age?"

"What's that?" he asked. "Just for the minute I happened to be thinking of all the papers I'd brought back in my case from the office."

"Poor darling" his wife cooed, in a genuinely soothing voice, while Miss Paynton was continuing to Peter,

"Terry's really rather sweet on the whole. He writes."

The boy gave a scared, hoarse laugh.

9

"Old Shone?" he cried. "Why, he's only the best half back we've had in fifteen years."

"But he does write poems all the same. Though I feel Terry rather lately's taken a wrong turning . . . "

"Are you feeling all right" the younger Middleton protested. "Here, have a glass of water, won't you? I mean, you must be having me on a bit. Because, since you say you do go down, and I've never even seen you, in the street that is, what sort of a meal do they stand people at their Lodgings?"

"Oh, fried eggs and all the rest."

"That's where the food goes, then!" the boy said, and looked moodily away.

"Well I call it very decent of you not to say straight out that I'm telling lies. For I do know him, you know, and visit." She wore a mysterious smile.

"You were a Prefect when you were at St Olaf's, surely Arthur?" Mrs Middleton interrupted.

"Of course" the man replied, and his son squirmed.

"Then did you have girls down from London in your day?" she enquired.

"Who else?" the father answered, at his most casual.

"Bet you couldn't have" was all Peter said to this.

"Don't contradict so, darling" Mrs Middleton protested. "Who ever heard of anyone being a Prefect at seventeen! It's absurd! And Arthur" she went on "poor love" she comforted. "Are you beginning to remember all that work? Can't you let it ride, just for this one evening?"

"My dear" he replied "I really do think we ought to eat now, if we're to get home in anything like reasonable hours."

"But we've ordered, Arthur! You know what these places are, my darling!"

"Why do you think I couldn't be friends with Terence Shone?" the girl pressed the young man again.

"No reason at all" he said in sulky tones.

"Because I am, you understand" she insisted.

"Well don't let him know you meet me, then! That's all I ask."

"We might possibly have other things to discuss" she assured Peter. "No, you needn't get worried" she added with a smile. "Honest, I shan't tell."

"I'm not the worrying sort" he said.

Then the parents' wine was served, Peter drank his shandy in one long soundless gasp and another was ordered, a dance band below struck up, soup was brought, and they began to seem as if they were enjoying themselves a little more.

"Oh it's so lovely to have you back" Diana exclaimed to her son. "Isn't it, Arthur?"

"This soup's marvellous all right" Peter announced. "Wonderful to be here" he agreed.

"Thanks to the soup!" his father laughed.

Peter laughed back. "If Ann will come down, so we starve . . . "

"But Peter!" Mrs Middleton cried out.

"I'd say they have to be bribed with all our food, the Prefects, or they'd never get anyone to take their job on."

"Oh, if you imagine I just go down to gorge" Miss Paynton laughed, dropped her spoon on the plate, and shoved the dish away.

"Then they must get all they do, just to spoil" Peter said, greedily eating.

"In an agony of despair about their figures?" Mr Middleton suggested.

"Haven't I already told you we needn't worry" the girl reminded him. He laughed. "Oh everyone eats too much" he insisted.

"But you can't at Peter's age. No boy can" Diana announced gaily.

"Oh Mother, now!"

"And so who's the greedy one?" Miss Paynton asked, delighted.

"Once my soup's gone, I'll be happy to take on yours" the boy proposed to Annabel, and winked.

"Go ahead. You're welcome" she replied.

"Oh Peter, no, you can't" his mother claimed in haste.

"But, my dear, why not?" Mr Middleton asked.

"In front of all these other people, darling?"

"Yet there's hardly anyone here" the husband pointed out, with truth.

"Go on, you disgusting hog" Annabel encouraged the boy with a fond smile. "And when you've your mouth full I'll make you laugh so you'll do the nose trick!"

"No, but honestly" Peter complained with what seemed great good humour, and leant across to take her soup plate.

"Because I've just had a bad go of trench mouth" she slyly added.

"That's done it" the boy said, then pushed her portion finally away.

"Oh you poor dear, you haven't" Mrs Middleton cried.

"And where did you learn about trench mouth?" the father demanded of the girl.

"From a cracked cup in her office canteen" his wife protested.

"All in all, that was probably a close shave" said Peter.

"But you don't really believe I've got it, really?" the girl wailed in mock despair.

"I'd heard those Prefects have been raising hell about their crockery lately."

"Now, see here Peter, I'll let you look into my mouth, if you wish. Why, only the other day, when I went to see him, my dentist said I had the most perfect gums."

"All right, let's have a peek, then" Mr Middleton demanded.

"Now Arthur, I've never heard such nonsense. No Annabel . . . !"

But, in spite of Mrs Middleton's appeal, the girl, with a 'here you are' leant over to the husband and opened wide the pearly gates. Her wet teeth were long and sharp, of an almost transparent whiteness. The tongue was pointed also and lay curled to a red tip against her lower jaw, to which the gums were a sterile pink. Way back behind, cavernous, in a deeper red, her uvula seemed to shrink from him. But it was the dampness, the cleanliness, the fresh-as-wet-paint must have made the man shut his lips tight, as, in his turn, he leant over hers and it was then, or so he, even, told his wife after, that he got, direct from her throat, a great whiff of flowers.

He drew back. He sighed. He shrugged his shoulders.

"Expect you'd pass in a crowd" he said at last.

"Here Peter" Annabel went on, and bent her head his side so the boy could see inside.

"God, thanks no" he exclaimed, then held his nose.

Annabel let out a peal of laughter. "You're the absolute limit" she complained.

"Really, my dears, you shouldn't" Mr Middleton said to all.

"I'm sorry but I properly asked for that, didn't I?" Miss Paynton exclaimed. "Look" she interrupted herself "there's Campbell Anthony come in."

"And who may he be?" Mr Middleton enquired.

"Only the best poet we happen to have."

"My dear Annabel, how thrilling! Where?" Mrs Middleton demanded.

The girl pointed out a most carefully dressed and neat young man who had just settled down below with another of his own age.

"Peter, let's dance" Miss Paynton quickly suggested.

"Not on your life" the boy said. "Besides my steak is due now, any minute."

"You're just a greedy brute" the girl laughed.

"He's no soul beyond his food, you'll find" Mr Middleton agreed. "But I'll try if you like, Annabel" he added.

"Why of course" she replied, after just a glance at the wife, and then they were gone.

Peter leant over the better to see them come out beneath, on the floor.

Diana laughed. "She only wants to show herself off a little before her poet" she translated.

At which moment their steaks arrived. "I don't think we need tell them to keep these hot" she said. "Let's eat ours and leave theirs get cold."

"Why not?" the boy echoed, already digging a fork in his. Then, for a while, they discussed what he should do in the holidays.

Arthur Middleton was dancing well, but not too close to Miss Paynton, over an almost empty floor.

"Nice of you to come out with us again" he said. "No great prize in all of this for you, I'm afraid."

"I wouldn't know what you mean" she replied. "Tell me, don't you think he looks quite terribly tired tonight?"

Mr Middleton saw she watched the poet.

"He could be not entirely fit" he agreed.

"Oh it's not that" she said. "Or, not always. Campbell will work so hard."

Arthur glanced down once more at the girl in his arms to catch her in a small nod of recognition sideways at the young man and also noticed that this Mr Anthony, who was busy talking, had missed it.

"How long hours does he labour then?"

"You see it's every day at the Ministry of Propaganda" she explained. "And now he's all taken up with this thing he's got on dance music so he has to go out to listen almost every evening – oh things are so exhausting and expensive for Campbell!"

"The writer's day is never done, you mean?"

"Why, quite" she replied.

They danced in silence through another few moments. Then Mr Middleton saw the poet at last wave negligently in their direction. Upon which, with a happy smile, Annabel Paynton moved closer within her partner's arms.

"Now, how awful of me" she exclaimed "I've just remembered! Peter says you simply slave at your business."

"Peter says?" he demanded, with some astonishment.

"Oh you've someone really special there, all right" she went on, enthusiastically bright. "He's going to be terrific."

"Well thanks" Arthur Middleton said drily.

"So here I go again" she lamented. "I suppose nothing can be a greater bore than having virtual strangers talk to one about one's own children."

"I wouldn't have thought we were quite that, Ann."

"No more did I, but you seemed . . . Oh I don't know, I expect I misunderstood. But I imagine people must be talking to you about Peter all the time."

"Not always" Mr Middleton smiled.

"Then tell me" she demanded. "D'you, yourself, get these awful depressions, too, from one day to the other?"

"Peter's never given me a moment's anxiety" he replied stoutly.

"No, no" she said "I thought you wanted to get off the topic of your son. I meant in yourself. Do you still have them?"

"Of course."

"But why? What's the purpose in one's always being depressed?"

"I should say it may have a lot to do with sex" he replied, with a nervous laugh.

She looked down her nose. "Would you?" she asked. "I wouldn't know, especially about sex, of course. No, Campbell worries so terribly over his health."

"You don't though, Ann. You look blooming."

"Yet I'm always in the dumps and there's nothing wrong with me, is there?"

"Not that I can see."

"And you say you do, as well? What is it, then?"

"The times, perhaps."

"But at the time everything has always seemed awful. You've only to read those bits in the newspapers quoting what they said a hundred years back. Their one idea is, the end of the world's in sight, even then!"

"What does Peter think about this?"

"But I mean he's much too young isn't he? Being a boy he's got at least another full two years to go yet, surely?"

"Oh, I was only curious to learn, if I could, whether he had these depressions too" Mr Middleton explained.

"Is that how things are by the time you have grown children?" she enquired. "That you're always more taken up with them than with other people?"

"No" he told her. "It's embarrassment, pure and simple, inclines one to lead any conversation back on them, away from oneself."

"Why away from you?"

"As they grow older they make you feel so aged."

"Oh I'm sure!" she obviously mocked. "But listen. Isn't this quite your favourite tune?"

"Well yes, rather" he admitted.

"I only wish everyone danced as well as you . . ." she said.

Up on the balcony Peter turned to his mother.

"Would you say she was having me on, when she made out she came down to St Olaf's to see Shone?"

"But why should she, darling?"

"That's exactly it. Annabel can't want to see him. He's not her brother."

"Oh well, you know Peter . . ."

"And she doesn't, in the least, care what position he holds in the School, you must admit."

"Perhaps she finds the boy attractive, dear."

Peter burst into happy laughter. "Oh now, that's absurd" he crowed. "Sorry and all that, but she couldn't. Why, she might even get him sacked!"

"It's no use going on at me!" his mother said equably. "Perhaps your Terence Shone is rich, has money."

"Oh, d'you think?"

"A girl's got to look after herself, you know."

"I'll bet!" He laughed. "Poor old Annabel! And to think she has to! Have you any idea when all this started?"

"Not the least. But I expect it could be very recent or, darling, you would be bound to have heard!"

"Yes I would" he solemnly agreed. "Marvellous steak" he added. At that moment the music stopped and the band filed out.

"Are they going to have meat, too?" he asked.

Arthur Middleton and Annabel came back gaily calling out for their own steaks, all laughter, and it was plain they were delighted. At which Peter asked the girl,

"Is Campbell the Campbell Anthony that used to be at St Olaf's?"

"Yes, the identical one!"

"Oh he's hopeless, then! He left at the end of my second term. Everyone breathed a huge sigh of relief."

"So what?" Miss Paynton demanded.

"Nothing" the boy replied.

"Steak's cold" Mr Middleton grumbled.

"Darling, Peter was so hungry" his wife explained.

An hour or two later Mrs Middleton, who had lit the coal fire in
her grate because it was chilly, waited in her double bed, waited for
Arthur with the lights off. At last she heard him coming, undress in
the bathroom and then, almost before she knew it she lay so
comfortable and warm, he was climbing cautiously between the
sheets.

"Finished darling?" she murmured when he had settled.

"All finished" he answered.

There was a pause.

"Asleep?" she asked in a low voice, without turning over towards
him.

"Not yet" he said.

"So wonderful" she immediately went on "really wonderful to
have Peter back! I'm afraid of burglars, alone in the house by
daytime."

"Stupid" he said and sighed with sleep.

"I know, darling" she insisted. "But I can't help myself. You don't
mind?"

"Course not" he muttered, then yawned.

"Such numbers of them" she continued in a reflective sort of
murmur. "Running through the house all day whenever it creaks.
You mustn't think I'm stupid to be nervous."

"Go to sleep" he whispered.

"I will, oh I will" she replied. "But I do love going out with you
and Peter so!"

"Me too" he said.

"Love it when he's back and dear Annabel" she continued.

"Sweet" he murmured.

"Poor darling, are you very tired?" she asked. On which he turned over on his back, watched firelight whispering on the ceiling while she rolled herself to his side and put a lazy arm warm across his throat.

"I'm so happy, dearest" she said.

"And so you ought" he answered.

"Just think of being her age again with this Terence Shone!"

"Questioned me if she should go on seeing him" he told her.

"Why didn't Ann ask me?" Diana wondered.

"Don't call her that. Annabel's the name."

"What Peter uses is good enough" the mother whispered.

"She doesn't like it."

"Who cares, darling?"

"Oh yes" he replied, mumbling agreement. "Who cares?"

"But I adore her" she went on. "The girl's fun, they laugh together."

Mr Middleton went "mm . . . mm."

"So good for Peter. And she's got no airs."

"Not a great deal to her" the man groaned.

Diana stirred. "I don't know how you can lie there and say that" she sleepily complained. "Why Annabel's sweet."

"I'll say" he agreed.

"Then are you a little bit enamoured of her darling?" In reply he laid a heavy fist across her legs.

"Stupid" he mumbled.

"Oh but I'm keeping you from your precious sleep" she exclaimed, her breath now a balm upon his neck. "Still it does amuse me terribly to see them together since she's almost grown up and he's such a tremendous schoolboy yet. You know there's lots of girls wouldn't at all be nice to him once they were 'out', in spite of having seen such a lot of each other when she was in the schoolroom."

"I'll bet" he mumbled.

"It is so" she insisted. "And frightfully good for Peter! Why I bless her. Believe me" she ended.

"Lucky young chap" he agreed, and yawned again.

"So well grown" his wife added.

"Wonderful" he mumbled.

"Oh I know you! I saw someone watching her!" she said. "And I do mean just a word of serious blame here, dear. It would be tiresome if Peter took it in his head to notice."

"Who're you referrin' to?"

"No one but you, Arthur darling. My wicked old darling. You won't too much, will you?"

"Dunno what you mean."

"You must go to sleep now, you're tired. Yes, you must. Go to sleep. Oh you'll never know how much I love you."

He snored.

"There, sleep darling" she murmured, she yawned.

A few days later Arthur Middleton, who had begun not to take a midday meal because he was getting fat, went to a News Film at one p.m. and ran slap into Annabel when he came out an hour later.

"I was just thinking of you" she greeted him.

"You were!"

"And how hard you worked!" she laughed.

"I skip lunch most days" he explained. "So once a week I go off in desperation to one of these places."

"Oh but oughtn't you to eat occasionally?" she cried. "You must be worn out by the time you get home."

"Well it seems to suit me. As someone once said, when you get to my age you can't digest any more, you simply ferment your food."

She laughed again. "Oh, don't you of all people start off by being disgusting!! And besides you aren't old! Whoever said so?"

"Diana for one."

"I'll bet she never can have."

"Look" he said. "We mustn't stand here like this all day, and hold up the foot traffic. Where are you bound for?"

"Well mine, thank goodness's as strong as an ostrich" she replied. "What's more I, for one, have to have food."

"Alone?"

"I am so it happens, yes, as a matter of fact."

"Then let me provide."

"Oh all right" she accepted without enthusiasm. "Yes, thanks."

He took Miss Paynton to the nearest expensive restaurant.

"You don't strictly need to spend all this amount of money" she exclaimed with more animation, brightening. "Really and truly" she added.

"Not every day I take you out."

"Yes, it's the first time alone" she agreed. "Oh don't allow them to put us anywhere but in the window! I might miss someone I know pass."

"I haven't any pull in this place" he warned her, but despite this modesty the headwaiter knew him by name, took a 'Reserved' card away, and sat them down where she could overlook the pavement.

"After anyone in particular?" he enquired.

"Who?" she vaguely asked, as though she had not heard.

"That you're looking for?"

"Why of course not" she grumbled. "Oh, but you are nice and kind to bring me here!"

"Because I've an idea that a certain Mr Shone doesn't live in London."

"You don't say! Oh now promise, you must, you can't think it awful of me to go down to see Terry" she pleaded, making her eyes very large at Arthur.

"My dear, it's not for me to stick my ugly nose into your affairs."

"Because I do get so terribly depressed sometimes" she explained.

"You are now?" he demanded in rather a gallant manner.

"But coming out as you did, you simply saved my life" she cried. "It was the luckiest thing! Just when I was so low I could hardly see out of my own eyes."

"Everyone gets fed up now and again, Annabel."

"What reason could you possibly have?" she protested. "You're married after all!"

"Yes."

"Well then!"

"Oh none, I suppose" he said, with some vagueness.

"Or do you think I shouldn't have expressed that last bit" Miss Paynton seemed to apologise. "I can't explain, only something made me bring to mind my grandfather, just now. He used to go out hunting twice a week, Mondays and Fridays, and travel back to the office Monday nights. And towards the end of his life he simply made a duty out of following hounds! Now that's absurd, isn't it? I mean what can it all have been but one more of his hobbies?"

"I don't hunt myself" Mr Middleton gently complained.

"Of course not" she agreed. "But just going to a cinema suddenly depressed you, you know it did!"

He smiled on the girl.

"You can't make out I look on that as a duty when I never do so more than an hour each week, at most."

"Don't assume everything so" she protested. "Or am I being an added curse on you? But dear Campbell says we wear ourselves out trying to fill in odd moments."

"How should I get through my lunch hour, then?" he asked. "Just continue to sit behind the old desk with clenched fists?"

"Well I don't see how you can pass the time if you can't eat and only go to the News Film once a week."

"Actually I walk round looking after all the pretty girls."

"Oh you don't!"

"Why not?"

"But it's . . . it's . . . it's wrong!! Mind, I'm not saying people never do, nice people I mean as well, only you've no earthly need, have you, you can't have like this, as you are, if you understand . . . "

"There's nothing wrong in that, Annabel" Mr Middleton complained.

"So you consider I'm just being childish!" she cried out, with a sweet expression of despair. "How then shall I ever explain? No, it's simply that you've no right to feel depressed, the happiest married couple in London and a lovely son whilst look at me, I've absolutely nothing, hopelessly in love with someone years younger than I am who's still at that beastly St Olaf's, me who'll probably never get married, ever!"

"You've still got everything in front of you."

"What good's that?" she cried. "It might turn out to be cancer."

"Oh come" he said. "Anyway I could have cancer in store for me, too."

"But you've had your whole life" she muttered.

"Oh well" he said drily. "Now let me try and get a waiter to carry on with our meal."

"You're bored" she accused him, with a pout.

It took some time to attract the man's attention. Miss Paynton meanwhile looked around the restaurant but did not seem able to hit on anyone she knew. During which, when Arthur Middleton casually began his story, she did not at first appear to listen.

"My office never opens Saturdays" he said. "When I rise up out of bed I go to buy the weekly Reviews, get some cigarettes for myself, change a library book and so on. Now you're familiar, of course, with the Arcade, aren't you? Three weeks ago I was just passing through when I saw a girl in a red coat coming, her eyes so hard on me they made me raise mine to hers. She really was rather pretty. Dark. Well I looked away, you know how things are – I thought she imagined she must have met me somewhere which I was fairly sure she hadn't, though I couldn't be quite certain – but when I took a second glance, by which time she was much closer, I saw she was still gazing full at me with a wonderful shy expression on her, but no smile if you follow what I mean. And then, when we came level, and I took a third look, she turned her face right away so I could see only the line of the jaw."

"And what was that like?" Miss Paynton demanded.

"Really rather terrific" he replied.

"Well, there you are then."

"If your suggestion is, she just wanted me to see the angle of her chin, then I can't agree. No I think she must have been watching in the reflection of a shop window."

Annabel laughed. "And did you speak to her?" she asked.

"That comes later" he explained. "So we passed each other like I told you" he went on "and I got the various bits and pieces I'd gone out to get. But when I was going back to my house, I passed by the Arcade once more, purely in case. And d'you know, there she still was, or anyway it was her again!"

"Well naturally."

"Why, you don't hang around like that yourself, Annabel?"

"I might."

"Is that the case? Anyway I wasn't so sure by this time I'd never seen the woman previously. I should have explained she had her back to me on this second trip but I recognised her, or thought I could, by the colour of the coat she had on and by a sort of droop to the shoulders I spotted when I'd seen the girl from in front; I can't explain, I don't know, it was submissive and patient, rather wonderful on the whole, attractive, – and as I was walking the faster, in the end I went by. I didn't like to turn my head but when I got to the street and had to go left I just looked round and there she was, standing at the greengrocer's, staring at me out of her huge eyes with all her heart!"

"And was she, all the time, this woman you'd already seen?"

"No, she can't have been, because I didn't spot her again till the Monday when I was waiting for my bus at the bottom of the Arcade. She came through and went across the road into the photographer's opposite, – you know the Polyphoto people."

"But what is it makes you think she can't have been the other woman?"

"Oh, if it had been Mary she'd never have gone into a Polyphoto. Besides this girl was in the selfsame coat!"

"But I believe you said you didn't know at all well this Mary you took her for."

"No more I do."

"Then how can you be so sure it wasn't the person it might have been."

"I can't say. But I am" he replied.

At this point their next course was brought them in a procession. They stayed silent until the waiters had departed.

"I hardly thought you were that kind" Miss Paynton said at last in a wondering voice.

"But I never spoke to her once" he objected.

"Somehow, though of course I don't know you at all well, I wouldn't have expected it" she murmured and did not look him in the eye. "Who could ever imagine you might turn out to be the sort to go chasing."

"Now Annabel" he protested "I wasn't." He seemed amused. "She was the one who did all" he defended himself.

"But it takes at least two to make a hunt, when everything's said and done, doesn't it?" she said. "The hounds and the foxes."

"In that case no man should ever go out of doors, even" Mr Middleton supposed.

"Well yes, perhaps so" she admitted. "Yet I do still think you were most to blame."

"For just looking at a strange woman, you mean?"

"When she was obviously trying to pick you up. Wasn't she?"

"I don't see it yet, Annabel. She may have spotted something about me which reminded her of someone, or even that she liked!"

"Of course it was the way I met Terry" Miss Paynton admitted in a dreamy voice.

"How? You just smiled in the street?"

"Yes. I'd gone down with some other people to see someone quite else."

"Well, where did I go wrong then?"

"Oh but you're married!"

"Just you wait until you are" he protested. "Can you see yourself out for a morning's shopping with your eyes on the flagstones like a young nun? I ask you!"

"Oh I know" she seemed to agree. "But I'd never, never tell a soul when I did the other."

"You still hold it's disloyal to one's wife or husband as the case may be?"

"Not exactly."

Mr Middleton studied the young woman, expressionless.

"What then?" he insisted.

"Well perhaps it makes one liable to be unlucky?" she suggested.

"In which way?" he asked, as if to drag this from her.

"The next thing could be your wife would, or my husband when I'm married."

"But it's life, dear" he said, with some impatience.

"Nothing will ever stop people meeting each other's eyes."

"Oh don't I know that!" she muttered. "Sometimes I could just strangle Terry; and at other boys, too, as he does. But, Campbell says, only to mention things makes them grow bigger."

"They grow far more from being kept secret, surely?"

"Oh I don't think that, I'm sure, at all."

"Then why say what you do about your Shone?"

"Because I love him" she replied at once, and immediately added "but I know I shouldn't speak it out loud."

"I can't see why you mightn't love him, Annabel. We're all human, after all."

"No, I mean about his catching other boys' eyes" she said. "I simply ought not to mention that again. I must remember!"

"But it can't matter if you do with someone my age, Annabel."

"I expect not. Oh I don't know. Come on" she said with a challenge. "Let's talk of doting. Tell me how you first met Diana."

"At a Hunt Ball" he told her, plainly reluctant.

"Well?" she insisted.

"That's so long ago now."

"So do go on" she urged. "It's become important for me to learn, all about first meetings."

"My parents had a party" he said. "They were alive then. We all went and I danced with Diana, of course, and the three other girls who were staying. I don't remember anything especial except, later on, I did notice the four of them had rather got together at a round table in the supper room and it seemed to strike me a bit that they weren't with any of our party any more, my two brothers I mean or the one other man we'd had down to stay, who was a Rowing Blue called Humphrey Byass. I saw the girls were pretty animated, not talking to the partners they were with at the time. But I don't think I thought much about it till next day, when the story broke."

"What'd happened?" Miss Paynton demanded.

"Well, I warned you, all this was quite a while back" Arthur Middleton explained. "It seems when Byass chose to dance earlier with one of our party, though not with Diana as it happened, he said the hair of her head had the most wonderful natural perfume."

At this point Mr Middleton paused as if at some enormity, and gave a bitter, embarrassed bark of a laugh.

"All right then, why not?" Annabel wanted to be told.

"You well may ask" he replied. "Anyway once we got back to the house about four in the morning and the girls went up to bed – they didn't; that is to say, while we were having a night cap down below, they hid themselves in Humphrey Byass' room, made an apple pie bed, filled his wash basin with water and balanced it on the open door, and so on."

"Was he cut about when it all fell down on him eventually?"

"Not in the way I expect you mean, yet he was a shy man and came to be considerably hurt. Left next morning, a day too soon."

"But I mean, how sad and odd!" Miss Paynton exclaimed. "What could be wrong with the poor boy's saying that?"

"Just the way Diana and I argued. We rather got together over the whole thing the following afternoon as a matter of fact, out shooting."

"Are you sure he didn't actually say a good deal more?"

"Not according to Diana. Of course she'd taken no part in the horseplay. Oh, how my wretched brothers were delighted! And the other girls would hardly speak to Diana after! Well, that was the start of Peter."

"All I can say is, I think your generation's extraordinary" Miss Paynton murmured. "Or was" she added.

"Of course we didn't have the boy till we'd been married a year, but it does seem strange what comes of things when one looks back" he said.

"No really!" Annabel protested. "Peter's sweet. And it's so undignified for him to have the whole of his having been born into this world, wished onto some old quarrel at a house party."

"You asked for it when you wanted to know how Diana and I first came to look at one another, after all!"

"So matter of fact" Miss Paynton grumbled.

"Well, did your parents ever tell you about themselves?"

"Now don't be horrible! Did yours?"

"Come to think of it, never" he admitted.

"All right then. So treat Peter like a human and not just an accident which came of someone else's apple pie bed."

"Here!" he demanded, the edge of anger on his voice. "I don't need instructions over my own boy. After all Diana and I were absolutely in the right."

"Now I'm being a real curse on you once more, aren't I?" she sweetly rejoined. "I'm so sorry! I got excited. Let's talk about other things, shall we?"

He was silent.

"I apologise. Was rude" she added in a low voice.

"I didn't want to start this, you know, Annabel."

"Of course you never did. It was all me. Let's get back to Mr Byass, Arthur. I mean, he simply must have said something else."

"Diana and I have often gone over it" Mr Middleton replied. "I don't now believe he can have done, even if you do think the others were very strange. Maybe he put his nose down into her hair for a moment while they danced. People weren't demonstrative in those days."

"I don't consider your generation is now."

"That's a matter of opinion" he commented drily. "But there's no question the other girls did take grave offence. And to take up your last remark I've often felt the incident stopped me afterwards paying those great luscious compliments to women which seem to be all the rage nowadays." He laughed selfconsciously.

There was a pause which she broke by saying, in the most natural manner,

"If I wished I could be married. Now! Any time I like!"

"Good" he replied.

"Yes, and to either of two people."

"Well, that's splendid Annabel."

"Oh, but not yet. All the same they both would propose any evening I let them." She was still speaking in a dreamy, reflective tone of voice.

"You don't wish them to yet, then?"

"I can't tell" she answered. "Perhaps I'm just waiting for something."

"What?"

"A sign like you two had over Mr Byass."

"But Annabel, Diana and I agreed about the others' behaviour."

"I bet your wife knew she was going to marry you."

He cleared his throat. "Now Annabel . . . " he began in a warning voice.

"I hate false modesty" she interrupted. "Any woman would be proud."

"It didn't come about the way you think in the least" he protested.

"Don't try to stop me blurting what I feel."

"Well thanks" he said bitterly.

"Or have I said something awful, yet once more?" she cried in what appeared to be scorn. "I just prefer men older. Can I help that? There, now you know my secret."

"Annabel, then you'll have to find a widower."

She gazed at Mr Middleton, large eyed. "Oh never. They're too cunning, must be" she protested. "But that's what's the fault with Campbell and Terry, so unformed!"

"You're going to have a job on your hands then."

She laughed at his last remark, "Isn't everything too tragic" she giggled. "Aren't I all kinds of a fool! But there it is, and nothing will ever change."

Soon after this he paid the bill and they left without arranging to meet again.

Some days later Annabel rang Peter Middleton and asked him out to lunch. They went to a cheap Indian curry place near where she worked.

"Did your father happen to mention he'd taken me out the other afternoon?" she enquired.

"No" the boy said in an uninterested voice. "Should he?"

"We ran across one another in the street. I'm afraid I can't afford anything like the gorgeous meal he provided."

"But curry's my favourite" Peter claimed. "I wish I had it every day. Decent of you to ask me."

"No, because I do truly enjoy seeing you. It takes me out of myself. And you've little idea how few there are I could say that of. Though, d'you know, it could be true about your Father. He's so terribly handsome, Peter."

The boy broke into mocking laughter, with his mouth full.

"Look out for the curry" she warned. "You'll blow it all over me and the table."

When he had composed himself he said,

"Well I once ate a green fig looked precisely like Dad's face."

She giggled. "Oh dear I suppose you could on the whole say that of him, some days" she admitted.

The younger Mr Middleton at this point changed the subject.

"I say" he said "you don't actually know Terence Shone do you?"

"You're talking now just like the boy out of a school story book" she objected. He grinned. "Of course I do. And he's not, anyway, so exciting a person as perhaps you might think. Come to that, he's dull as ditch water sometimes. I'm a bit off Terence. But I didn't ask you out to lunch to discuss private affairs. Let's go on more about your Father. Look, I'll tell you about mine if you wish."

The boy seemed to pay not the slightest attention.

"Are your parents still in love?" she asked.

"My mother and father? God, I suppose so. Are yours?"

"Not a bit. No."

Peter went on eating.

"They don't even share a room" she added.

"D'you mind?" he asked at last.

"Well it makes things rather wearisome at times" she said. "They have endless rows, going into the same old grouches over and over again. What's so extraordinary is, they never seem to say anything different. Are yours like that?"

"Well I expect they are Ann, yes. Of course I'm not home much, only in the holidays. They're pretty average I should say."

"How long have they been married?"

"Lord, don't ask me. I wouldn't know."

"All in all I'd imagine they were still very much in love" she suggested.

"I expect so" he said.

"You won't tell them I mentioned this, will you?"

"What d'you take me for?" he protested. "I don't discuss anything with my parents."

"And can't you, then, ever talk over your own father" she demanded suddenly with some petulance.

"On occasions" he replied with calm. "At St Olaf's."

"Why there?"

"Didn't you go to school?"

"No" she said. "I had governesses."

"Wouldn't you discuss your parents with them?"

"Heavens" she cried with a shrill laugh. "You've never seen mine or you couldn't say that."

"No" he agreed. "I'd be too young."

"I don't think you are, Peter. It wasn't such ages ago. I say, in your own mind, would you consider your mother beautiful?"

32

"Yes" he said, rather gruff, "as a matter of fact."

"Me too" she echoed, but in a sad little voice. "She has everything. Hair, teeth, skin, those wide apart eyes. By any standard your father's a very lucky man."

"Why?"

"To have such a wife of course. Would you say she liked me, Peter?"

"Fairly, yes. No reason not to, is there?"

"Oh none" she agreed, casually.

"She was jolly pleased with you as a matter of fact for coming along again the other night, to the play and afterwards."

"But I loved to, Peter."

"Shouldn't have thought it could have been much fun for you."

"I adore them both, you see."

"Well look out then, Ann! If you go on being so intense about it, you'll get nerves or something."

At which they began to giggle at themselves, then over the Indian waiter who was a melancholy looking man, at the hot curry and saffron coloured rice, and then over the sweet which looked like little dog's turds, under the pink paper carnations in a dry, dusty vase.

The same evening Arthur Middleton worked as usual on the papers he'd brought home from the office. When he did come at last he found the fire lit, lights extinguished and Diana in bed, humped beneath the clothes, motionless, hardly breathing.

He undressed quietly, as usual, and climbed with stiff knees between the sheets. Mrs Middleton again had her broad back toward him, the dark hill of her thigh was across his sight.

"Finished darling" she murmured, when he had settled down.

"All done" he mumbled.

There was a long pause.

"Gone off yet?" she asked in a low voice.

"No, my dear" he replied.

"Wasn't it sweet of darling Annabel" she said.

"What's the girl done now?"

"Taken Peter out to lunch."

"Did she" he murmured in an uninterested voice.

"So good for him at his age" Diana added.

Mr Middleton gave a grunt.

"I daren't think what they can have found to talk about, though" Mrs Middleton wondered. "Of course I chatter away to him and he's so jolly with me always – that's only natural, but wasn't it generous of anyone in her generation to take the trouble?"

"Yes indeed" he faintly assented.

They were lying back to back. Diana turned over, settled the sheets about his chin. He brought a hand up and put these back the way they were.

"Sleepy?" she murmured.

"A bit" he admitted.

"Well you can talk just a few minutes more" she said, in almost a brisk voice. "What d'you think they find to say to one another?"

"Discuss us?" he suggested.

"Oh we'd have no earthly interest for them, Arthur. Besides darling Peter would be too loyal."

"Children do compare notes, you know."

"Dig out things in common between me and Paula Paynton. Oh, no dear!"

He mumbled unintelligibly.

"What Arthur?"

"Only saying I've not much in common with Prior Paynton either."

"Oh, that fool of a man" she said. "There could be no earthly resemblance at all, darling."

With a slow heave Arthur Middleton levered himself over on his back. Diana rearranged the sheets under her chin. Firelight whispered on the ceiling.

"Well I can't say what the children discuss" he admitted in quite a strong voice. "Anyway, it won't be wine women and song, not at his age."

"But d'you think she could be a little old for him, Arthur?"

"You just said . . . "

"Now I'm asking you, dear" she interrupted.

"What exactly is it you mean, Di?"

"Of course it's good for Peter to see life, but I was wondering if I liked his going out, quite so soon, with older girls."

"Jealous of Annabel, darling?" Mr Middleton enquired with a smile.

"Well yes, I suppose I am, perhaps, a bit."

"But Di, this has got to come sooner or later with the boy."

"I'm not sure, you see, if this is not too soon. I don't mind your asking her out to lunch, of course, as you did when you ran into the child, but don't you understand, she couldn't have you back, she had to invite Peter instead. And those beastly, cheap curry places are dangerous with the food they serve. Besides he might get hashish there, or hemp, or whatever it is these Indians take."

"Oh my love" he said "no! I promise they're most respectable."

"All of them?"

"Certainly."

"Every single one?"

"Well of course, Di, I couldn't say."

"There you are then . . . "

"So I mustn't ask out anyone we've entertained here, to come to lunch, if I stumble into them on the street, for fear they may invite Peter to a meal in return? Is that it?"

She chuckled.

"Yes" she said.

He laughed.

"I see" he said.

"Do you, Arthur?"

"Well yes. In a way" he answered.

"Which means you aren't going to pay the slightest attention?" She laughed with great good humour. "Is that what you mean, my wicked old darling?"

His reply was to turn over and give her a light kiss on the nose.

"Well, you may be right, though I'm sure not" she said. "I expect you think I'm just being silly."

"I love you" he murmured, shutting his eyes.

She put a lazy arm warm across his throat. He laid a heavy fist over her legs.

"There, sleep my darling" she mumbled.

And in a moment or two he snored.

Some days later Mr Middleton rang Annabel first thing, soon as he got to the office.

"Oh it's you" she answered in a neutral voice when he reached her.

"Look" he continued. "I don't know how you expect a man to pass his lunch hour, but I was wondering if you wouldn't do me a favour and come out, for once, today?"

"To lunch?" she asked in an expiring voice. "Well, I might."

"Same time and place?" he enquired in what seemed elaborately casual tones.

"Oh yes, very well. Yes, thanks a lot" she said.

Yet, when they met in the restaurant, she was all smiles.

"This is sweet" she said in her clear piping voice, and seemed to draw Arthur forward while shaking his hand. "And in this glamorous, expensive room again. You are kind!"

"Nice of you to turn up" he answered.

"Why, I'm not late, am I?" she asked. "Oh, if you only knew" she added without waiting for the reply, preceding him to the bar.

"What?"

"Simply no one invites me anywhere, any more" she complained.

"Rot."

"No longer now, it isn't, alas," Annabel insisted, then had three cocktails, one after the other.

So it was with sparkling eyes that she reached their corner table, in the end. This time they didn't overlook the street.

"I've been through such dire trouble with Mummy" Miss Paynton began, as soon as they had ordered.

"Not the first or the last time I presume" he smiled.

"No" she said "but this is serious. Of course I'm really much closer to Mummy than I am to Dads but I can't remember her ever being so cross with me, ever before."

"What about?"

"You see I went down to visit someone in the country."

"Shone?" he asked.

"Well yes" she said. "For the first and only time, as a matter of fact. And Terry's parents turned out to be really quite odious people. So rude, when I did go as a guest, after all!" ·

Miss Paynton made her eyes very large and round at Arthur.

"Oh quite" he said with an encouraging smile.

She began to giggle.

"Terry didn't altogether invite me" she went on. "But when he phoned and wanted to know what I was doing with myself these days, I said 'why on earth don't you just come up to London for an evening?' and he said he simply hadn't the money. Oh Arthur" she cried, using his Christian name for the second time, "how squalid it can be to fall in love with a schoolboy! So then I had to journey to him! I made Bill Allen take me in his car."

"Who's he?"

"Nobody. He has a big car. I bet Mrs Shone was surprised to see me in anything so terrific."

"How old is this Allen?"

"About twenty four. What's that got to do with it?"

"Nothing" Arthur said. "But you've this to consider; if you were both young then Mrs Shone could have been seized with jealousy, Ann."

"Well of course. She can't expect to be any other way from now on, can she?"

"Unless she does you down, in the end."

"Oh how beastly even to dare suggest such a thing" Miss Paynton exclaimed while she smiled fondly on Arthur. "What'll you bet?"

"No thanks" he smiled back. "You can't be serious, though, when you say you expected a warm welcome from this woman."

"Did I say that?" she objected. "Because it turned out, in the end, Terry had been too frightened to tell his mother we were coming. So Bill and I couldn't have done worse when we roared up the drive in good time for lunch. It's a Dagonda. In addition to which, Sunday comes as a very quiet day for them down there. But you must agree, all in all, it was perfectly disgraceful on poor Terry's part."

"Well, I can't entirely see that."

"If you'd only heard him on the phone! He sounded so low, poor dear."

"Which is the only one reason you felt you had to go?"

"Why else?" she asked.

"And the father then? What sort of a man is Mr Shone? Didn't he like you?"

"Oh, he's much older than you."

"I thought you once said you preferred older men!"

"Terry's father would be too sweet if he wasn't so dim with his wife" Miss Paynton answered with a bright smile. "But although there wasn't enough for his lunch because of Bill and me, I could tell he was quite thrilled. The worst of all this was, Sunday is a considerable day for them into the bargain, as I said before. They go to church and that."

"Yes" Arthur agreed. "Granted."

"But I'm a bit off Terry at the moment" she went on. "I was, already, if you remember, a week or two back, only for a different reason. Then when Bill had to lug me down halfway to the sea, all that distance and he can't afford it any more than Terry can, coming up to London, well, I mean, I don't see how I could be expected to stretch my loyalties between two boys as if I was a bit of wonderful elastic, do you?"

"I'm sure you gave joy to Shone, anyway."

"That might be" she agreed. "But if only he wasn't so meek" she answered. "He was struck dumb at not having told his mother about lunch. That's what must have brought all the stuffiness out in her. Oh" she said, and her eyes filled with bold tears, "isn't everything really too terrible, sometimes? One goes down to the rescue of a fellow human being of whom one's frightfully fond at the moment, he sends out an S.O.S. for help, and they treat you like a thief, a baby snatcher."

"The best way" Arthur said "is to give advice only over the telephone and then never find out if the advice has been taken. Above all, don't follow up in person."

"In that case how's a girl ever to get married?"

"In what way, d'you mean?" he asked.

"I hope I never fall so low as to receive my proposals, if I should get any, on long distance, with women in every exchange between where he is and London comparing notes on how he pops the question."

"Yes, I see" Arthur admitted. "I suppose you must face the men concerned."

"In the end I imagine the one thing will be to fall in love just with those one can meet naturally, without all this perfectly ruthless parent trouble."

"Your men would need to be much older, then."

"Yes, they would" she agreed with a smile. "Arthur, you're sweet. In fact I don't know how I'd manage without you, and Diana, and dear Peter. But what made it worse was, when I told Mummy of the disastrous trip down to see, she turned quite cross and said I oughtn't to have gone! Well I realise the way her mind works, how she looks at things through her generation's spectacles, but you do understand, don't you, I can't sit at home and simply wait, can I? Not as things are now."

"Why not?" he argued. "You've loads of time."

"There never is" she objected, and again her eyes filled with tears.

At this point the wine waiter came to take their order. Mr Middleton laid knife and fork down.

"Will you have anything, Ann" he asked.

"Oh no thanks" she answered with a sad smile. "Just plain water, please."

"D'you mind if I take a whisky and splash?"

"How could I when you're being so perfect."

Arthur ordered the drink.

"You are inclined to flatter one a bit, you know" he said when they were alone once more.

"Me?" she cried. "All I can say is, I wish you were my parent."

"What about your own father, then?"

"Dads?" she said. "Oh he's sweet right enough. But Mummy and me don't see such a lot of him just now."

"I know" he gravely agreed. "I'd heard something. Your parents are two of Diana's oldest friends."

"Are now, or used to be?" she asked.

"Yes" he admitted "things can't have been easy for you since Prior and Paula began not to get on. Unhappy people are apt to be bores, Annabel."

"That's exactly what so terrifies me about myself" she exclaimed. "I can't ever be sure, now, I'm not becoming one. Peter's lucky to have you, believe you me. Because, as you've just hinted things are truly a bit grim for us at home at the moment, so I have to watch myself the whole time to guard against the utter bore I may become."

"What absolute rot" he protested. "Of course you aren't."

"Oh, but yes!"

"Yet you've two young men up your sleeve, ready and glad to propose tomorrow."

"I told you" she said. "They don't mean a thing."

"But, Annabel, they must prove to you that you're liked."

"I expect they only go to show I'm not entirely hideous" she muttered.

"Don't sit there across from me and say your generation of males want to marry just because a girl's a good-looker, for I simply won't believe that" he pronounced.

"Well, what d'you know about it?" she asked politely.

"In my time people didn't."

"Of course you in particular never could" she agreed at once. "But if what you say is true, then how lucky you both are, don't you understand, I mean with the person you married."

41

"No, honestly Annabel, if you're trying to make out men of your own age can't fall genuinely in love any longer, then I give up."

"You see" she replied "you were all so much more high principled in your day. From your own lips I had that story about a Mr Humphrey . . . Humphrey what's his name?"

"Byass. How does he come into this?"

"Yes Byass. Well those girls, as they were, just must have mobbed the man because they thought he wasn't genuine."

"Good Lord no! I don't think that at all. They were only being objectionable and hearty. You can't make them out to be more than they were."

"What have you ever known about women?" she demanded with some petulance.

"Enough never to discuss 'em" he drily replied.

"Yet you do all the time, probably."

"Perhaps it's only when I'm with you" he suggested, smiling.

"Now I'm boring you once more" she exclaimed in obviously mock contrition. "But I do apologise" she said with a sort of humble rage. Then Miss Paynton added, self pityingly, "What a way to entertain one's host over luncheon!"

"Nonsense" he said, in what, it seemed plain, was some alarm. "Exciting for a man my age to be out with anyone as pretty as you."

She left her eyes on his face and looked sad.

"Care was taken in those days" she said. "Girls were looked after, you yourself protect them still. I don't mean only you, but your whole generation."

"Perhaps it is girls won't take the trouble, now" he suggested.

"Don't take trouble?" she echoed with indignation.

"Oh you mustn't think I can't realise how good you are to come out and bother with me" he put in quickly "but I . . ."

"Please stop now, at once, being so modest" she interrupted. "I'm sure you can't mean that. I like to be invited by you. I dote on when you ask me. Now then!"

"All right, thanks. I'm sorry" he said. "But you'll ruin your whole life, believe me, if you insist that everything was better in the days you're too young to remember. People don't change much and if one wanted to find them distasteful then, it used to come quite easy."

"How can I wish to dislike anyone?" she pouted.

"Well, if I may say so, you're going the right way about it now."

"Why? I'm kind to everybody."

"Kindness doesn't count, Ann."

"Sometimes I think I'm too nice" she went on as though she had not heard. "I know Mummy thinks so. She says I shouldn't try to comfort people when they get miserable."

"I suppose it's a question of degree" he said.

"Well they will ring up, and will be desperate, and then I manage to go round, or motor down if I possibly can. Could any fellow human do less, Arthur?"

"Isn't Shone a bit young to be getting so desperate?"

"Oh I wasn't thinking of Terry just for the moment. No, sometimes, when Campbell's distracted, he telephones, when he's stuck in his work, and so on."

"What's he at now?" Mr Middleton asked.

"An anthology of love poetry he's to call 'Doting'. Don't you agree it's a marvellous title?"

"Well, you know doting, to me, is not loving."

"I don't follow" she said with a small frown.

"To my mind love must include adoration of course, but if you just dote on a girl you don't necessarily go so far as to love her. Loving goes deeper."

"Well" she suggested "perhaps the same words could mean different things to men and women."

"Possibly" he said. "Perhaps not."

"So anyway, quite often, Mummy and I are sitting alone after dinner, and you can be sure her poor heart is full of where Dads is, and then the phone rings so that we race each other. I always win. After which, as likely as not, it only turns out to be Campbell who's got stuck in his work, and wants my company."

"Yes" Mr Middleton admitted. "I sympathise with you. Things can't be easy back home at present."

"You are sweet, you really are. Am I being an awful bore?"

"Of course not. But tell me, how can this Campbell get stuck over an anthology?"

"Well, it wouldn't be cut and dried to choose among so many poems after all."

"So he reads them out to you for your opinion?"

"Oh no, we play records, as a rule, to take his mind off. He has this thing, too, about jazz, you see."

"So I understood" Mr Middleton said, in a wondering voice.

"But he can't listen alone."

"Why not?"

"Campbell says jazz is written for crowds and so mustn't be heard if you're one in a room."

"I see. Then has he asked you yet to share his loneliness for good?"

She frowned. "I don't think that's very nice at all" she said. "It might be almost nasty" she added in a sad voice "or else you're not so understanding as you seem. But of course Campbell would love to live in sin with me and I might adore it too, yet I'm not going to. Although, as I said, he could really be rather wonderful."

"I'm sorry" Arthur apologised. "I was confused."

"What about?"

"Everything Ann."

"Who's to blame you" she suddenly laughed. "Look at me! I get so tangled up over my own feelings I often don't know where I am myself."

"Wouldn't it help to talk this over with your mother, then?"

"I couldn't bother Mummy now, just when she's so worried."

"And yet, that might take Paula out of herself, a bit" he suggested.

"In which case you don't know my mother" she said. "Anything about me could only be yet another great worry for her."

"Yes I see. All right. But to go back to what you were saying, Annabel. Aren't you taking things too seriously? Because you needn't think your emotional life will ever not be in a tangle, dear."

"You say I'm so crazy I shan't once be able to snap out of it?" she demanded with what appeared to be humble indignation.

"Of course not" he pleaded with her. "Take my own case, now, for example. Half the time I don't know where I am, in my emotional life I mean, whether I'm coming or going."

"If you ask me seriously to believe that" she objected "then all I can say is your memory must be short, or else you intend to forget. I don't know the sort of life you used to lead but, just for a minute, look back to what it must have been before you married and had Peter."

"I often do."

"You do!" she cried. "And you say you're worse off at the moment? Well, of course, I'm sorry" she corrected herself "that's not your argument, but you maintain, because this is what you're saying, isn't it, that you have a worse time now than me who's simply got no one, or anything!! Or have I gone too far again?" she asked in a contrite voice. "Still, I don't feel you can remember properly. Because I won't agree. So long as I live, I won't!"

"The fact is" he explained with calm "the minute one begins a discussion of mutual troubles or miseries, it invariably becomes a kind of fierce competition as to who, in effect, is the worse off."

"Well, why not?"

"But Ann, I was just trying to help."

"I'm sure you were, only how?"

"What I was after was an attempt to show that you were not alone in your old boat."

"Even if I wasn't, in which way would that alter things?" she demanded.

"Then you won't have any comfort?"

"What do you mean?" she muttered with a lost look. "Here you are, married with a lovely son, what can the matter be?"

"How about your own parents, then? There's plenty wrong with them."

"But you're happily married!"

"Are you trying to make out you know, better than I do, what's the matter with me?"

"Well, all right, then" Miss Paynton crossly announced. "And to think that you even own your own house" she added. "But, because you at least see I do realise what my trouble is, just admit, then, I've simply no one, and nothing."

"I remember a working man once said to my face 'what have you to worry about, you're rich'" Mr Middleton told the girl.

"Oh, how could I mean money?" she protested.

"I don't either" he assured her.

"But you must understand" she protested. "Compared with my case you're well off beyond the dreams of avarice." Then she laughed. "Or perhaps not beyond my dreams" she added, suddenly gay. "Because, of course, I do want such a vast great deal."

She leant across and squeezed his hand on the table cloth. Then changed the subject. She began to take infinite pains, and soon had him smiling at a long story about one of her girl friends.

When it was time for her to go back to work she said "Do please ask me again. You've done such a lot of good. Promise!"

"I will, if I may" he replied as he raised his hat.

That same evening Mr Middleton worked as usual, after dinner, in the study, while his wife sat with Peter in the living room of their flat. The boy was seated opposite Diana on a sofa with the whole day's newspapers piled around him, the sheets separately strewn about to left and right halfway up to his shoulders. Two table lamps were lit, one for Mrs Middleton to read by in her armchair and the other, so placed as to command the empty chair sacred to his father between this sofa and the fire, gave the boy but little light, although he had tilted the shade so that the bulb shone into his mother's eyes. And, as he was done with the day's news, he now breathed heavily over a catalogue of gramophone records.

"Why don't you change to where Arthur always sits, darling?" Mrs Middleton suggested. "Then you'd be able to see better."

"But he'll come back any time" the young man replied.

"I don't think so, not yet" she said. "He does work so hard, he has such a lot to do. Because you'll ruin your eyes like this."

"No I won't."

"What's the matter with you tonight?"

"Nothing. Why?"

"Oh Peter, are you getting bored with London again?"

"Not more than usual."

"Where would you like to be, then? In the country?"

"Well it might make a change."

"We go through this every holidays" she lamented. "But there's no one to visit! And hotels are so expensive. Look, if you're desperate why won't you take someone out? I'm not sure you're old enough yet but I've my number two account for your expenses, and I'd provide the wherewithal."

"There's no one to go with."

"How about Annabel?"

"Oh, not her!"

"Then why don't you ring up one of your school friends? What are they there for? Some of them must live in London."

"God no."

"Which doesn't exactly make anything easier, does it?" Mrs Middleton commented ruefully. "Peter, don't say you have something against Annabel now?"

"When did I ever even like her, Mother?"

"But she's been such a companion for you all these long years!"

"Well there are chaps at St Olaf's say they don't particularly care even for their sisters."

Diana laughed. "Yes" she agreed "I can remember my brothers were the same. Still Annabel does adore you, darling. Why, she took you out only last week!"

"That was no more than to pay Father back for all he had spent."

"And I don't think so" Mrs Middleton protested, in an unconfident way. "In any case Arthur asked her out to lunch this afternoon. You wouldn't wish to rely on her inviting you again, surely?"

"He did? He does see quite a bit of her now!"

"Why shouldn't your Father stand lunch to whosoever he likes?" Diana enquired patiently. "I'm glad he can relax at times, with all that work of his."

"But, I mean, Ann's young enough to be my sister."

"That's no reason for him not to invite the child, is it?"

The boy gave a disdainful hoot, at which Mrs Middleton laughed a bit, with a show of confidence. "I know your Father" she said. "You must at least allow me that. Nonsense!"

"Well I think it's silly at his age."

"Now Peter, I'm not going to have you get tiresome over the holidays. Oh I realise it can't be easy here in London but we've nowhere else to go that we can afford, have we, and in any case this is not the right time of the year for shooting."

"No, I know."

"You've got to learn to take your pleasures where you find yourself" she went on equably. "You can't suppose I like to sit here alone, while you're away, night after night, with Arthur at work downstairs."

"Well, why does he?"

"Someone's got to earn the money to keep you at school and pay for all this, Peter."

"But doesn't he invite you out to lunch sometimes?"

"Of course. Yet, if he wants to ask Ann, one's only too pleased that he should be getting his mind off a bit. Now why don't you take your gun to the shooting school and put in some practice?"

After which they cheerfully discussed this and other methods for him to get through the holidays, till it was time for bed.

The next Monday Arthur Middleton was sitting opposite Miss Paynton at the same corner table of that restaurant they used every week for lunch.

"Now we've established a habit by coming here, what shall we talk about?" he gaily enquired.

"Tell me of when we first met" she said.

"You were six."

"Go on. Then how was I dressed?"

"With a pink bow in your hair."

"Oh I expect. But which time of day was it?"

"Lunch."

"Well, don't stop. What frock did I wear?"

"I'm sorry but all this was a long time now. Twelve whole years, you know."

"I can remember all my dresses" she replied. "Then how did we talk?"

"Di was busy with Prior and Paula, whilst I sat next you" he began. "We discussed cleaning our teeth and got on, when no one was looking, to making terrible faces at each other."

She sniffed. "That doesn't sound terribly exciting" she announced.

"Can't you really remember, Ann?"

"But there's nothing to remind me, surely?"

"No, I meant before lunch that day. The rabbit hutch."

"All this is news to me" she assured him. "And you mustn't expect a girl to bring to mind everything. That was so long ago."

"Well, thank God" he said, in what seemed a strained voice. "I know I shan't ever forget and I've been afraid all these years you might have taken a turn!"

"What is all this?"

"You see, you brought me out alone with you before lunch, to inspect your rabbit."

"Nip? Or Tig? No, this must have been earlier. Why you can't mean Doughnut?"

"How should I remember at this distance?"

"Well, continue Arthur. Tell!"

"It was a big rabbit and a large hutch" he began with obvious reluctance. "About three feet off the ground. You'd fixed a sloping plank so that when you turned your Doughnut out he wouldn't have to jump down. D'you recall where the hutch was, because that's everything. In the ruined chapel, on a lawn which used to be the floor, the greenest grass. I suppose you could get used to most of it but the walls, the extraordinary brick and blue ivy and stillness, absolutely not a sound, because I remember the sun was very strong that morning – well, I imagine, I shan't ever forget your rabbit twitching its nose at you while you got down on hands and knees to show me how it had to climb to get back. I thought the ladder would break under your weight, it was only elm. Then you clambered on top of the hutch, to simply become your rabbit. You crouched on the roof to show me how Doughnut, or however it was called, crouched, and the damn animal was beneath you all the time so I thought the whole thing must collapse under your weight and kill the wretched thing. All of which made me say for you to come down, but you paid no attention, and, in the end, I caught hold of your ankle to pull you off but, Ann, you screamed! Can't you remember?"

"How stupid" she commented. "Why on earth should I do that?"

"It was most significant" he gravely said.

"So what?" Miss Paynton asked.

"You yelled like a stuck pig. I thought your parents would be on me in a flash."

"Why Arthur?"

"Well I did have your ankle in my fist. You wore blue cotton socks."

"I'll bet I didn't. Not blue at any age."

"Yes, it is so. I shan't ever forget."

"And so, then?" she demanded. "After all, what makes this very serious?"

"Embarrassment, Ann" he replied.

"Good God" she said. "Then you are really a mass of nerves inside?"

"I'm allergic to children if you want to know."

"You mustn't even pretend you are about your Peter."

"I am with little girls" he said, in a satisfied voice.

"Up to what age?" Miss Paynton asked.

"Now don't you poke fun at me" he said, and changed the subject.

That same week, on a summer evening, Mr Middleton walked a friend home from his club.

"No, but what do you really think about them?" he was persisting.

"Not much" Mr Addinsell replied.

"All right" Arthur Middleton admitted. "But one thing you must agree, that they simply wave it about in front of one."

"Females always have and will" his companion said.

"You know what happened to me? Took my wife out with this girl and she leans on a balcony on purpose so I can look right down the front of her dress."

"What might her name be?" Mr Addinsell demanded.

"Is none of your damned business" Arthur Middleton laughed. "But things are very different now, aren't they, to when we first went out in London."

"I don't know, I wouldn't be too sure" his companion demurred.

"Meaning I could be at the dangerous age, Charles? Oh well, all the same, really young girls never have behaved like that in the whole history of the world."

"What do you care, after all?"

"Because she's simply destroying me, the little tart" Mr Middleton sang out in indignation. "I can't sleep at night any more when I think of her" he said. "In a week or two I'll even be obsessed."

"Oh get it over with, Arthur, and go to bed with the child."

"I could, of course, with a bit of luck, only I'm so upset it might make me worse. But Charles, your own boy's only eight, isn't he?"

"Rising nine, Joe. What difference is there in that?"

"You see this little bit is the one we almost always bring along, each time we take Peter out and about London. She's nineteen, or a trifle over."

"Well then, she's two years ahead of him, isn't she?"

"About that. But look here, I wouldn't! You must see that. I couldn't! Not with the girl we trot out for Peter."

"You'd get between the sheets in five years' time with your boy's own wife, if I know you, old man" Mr Addinsell guffawed. "Yet why d'you suppose Diana asks this nameless young lady along? Tell me."

"I've told you already. To bring the lad company."

"Not on your life Arthur. The purpose is to keep you gay."

Mr Middleton gave a snort. "But not for me to be gay in bed with, you can count on that."

"Perhaps you may be right there" Charles Addinsell admitted. "Still, I've never known such a trifle hold a good man down before, not yet at all events."

"The girl never would."

"How can you tell, Arthur, if you haven't tried? There's all sorts of things come into bed, where they're concerned, at their age. Curiosity for one. Impatience. Anything. And then, they imagine men as old as we are won't be a bother afterwards."

"I suppose I do seem like a grandparent in her eyes."

"So what? When you were nineteen didn't you consider your aunts' lady friends?"

"No, honest to God, I don't think I did."

"Then you were the only one, is all I can say."

"Now Charles, what would you do if you were in my shoes?"

"Run like a hare."

"There you go again" Mr Middleton laughed. "Can't you ever be serious?"

"I'd have to meet the sweet little thing first, Arthur."

"God forbid, where you're concerned, old man. And yet, in the end, you'd simply make yourself scarce if you were me, is that it?"

"You alarm me Arthur, that's all. You're losing sleep over this, you say?"

"I am a bit."

"And you, so serious as you've always been about your damned work. No, you just listen. Run like a hare."

"I might, at that" Mr Middleton said. "But, somehow, I don't think I can."

Her day's work done, Annabel Paynton had a drink in the pub outside the office with her confidante, Miss Claire Belaine.

"Oh Claire" she said. "Can you imagine, but it's happened again!"

"Another?"

"Yes. Don't laugh. He's married and middle-aged."

"Well, that does make for a bit of variety!"

"There! You are laughing. I knew you might" Miss Paynton rather breathlessly exclaimed although her companion, who was short and fat and ever wore an expression of comfortable wisdom, did not even smile. "All right, then, just wait till this happens to you, Claire. Everyone has their turn."

"I will. What's his name?"

"I don't think it would be fair to tell."

"Have I met him?" Miss Belaine demanded.

"Shouldn't think so" Miss Paynton said, after which there was a pause.

"So you say he's married?"

"Of course."

"So are you in love with the man?"

"But Claire how can one tell, and when I've not described a thing about him yet?"

"I'm sorry. Go on, darling."

"It's simply I'm very much afraid the whole old rigmarole is about to start all over, once more."

"Like Terence, or like Campbell you mean?"

"No. This one's so much older, you see."

"Well, in that case, avoid getting tangled with the wife then, Ann."

"But sometimes I'm terribly sorry for him, darling."

"Why? Does he complain?"

"Never! Arthur's not that sort at all."

"Arthur?"

"There I go! My dear darling, you're to forget I ever once let the name slip. In any case you can't know, can you? I mean there are so many middle-aged Arthurs. But should one stop oneself being sorry for people? I don't see how one could, do you? Seriously, are we to go round, for ever, just being careful against our truly better feelings, or judgements?"

"Well then, exactly what d'you expect to get out of this?" Miss Belaine asked judicially.

"How should I know? Ought we to reckon on a profit?"

"You might lose."

"But, Claire, I don't think so; only why not, if it comes to that? Because these endless Campbells and Terences just don't exist yet, they haven't even any feelings still, they're damp. All they do is to use you with their parents. One's an excuse to borrow the car."

"Won't this Arthur make use of you, whoever he is?"

"I expect he will" Miss Paynton laughed. "But Claire, look, at our age we must be fairly expendable."

"Why?"

"Simply because we have our own lives to make and you just can't prepare for that dressed in white muslin, a dummy in the shop window, the wonder bride-to-be."

"How serious are you, Ann? You wouldn't invite me to meet him?"

"The only thing is, we can't see each other except where he has to pay."

"Hotels?"

"Restaurants" Miss Paynton replied with a kind of satisfied calm. "And that's one thing in his favour. One does get the most delicious food. Not like sitting over a tired sandwich with poor Campbell, to listen to a cheap band, thanks very much."

"Well, everyone to her own taste, Ann."

"Then you do think it dreadful in me?"

"All I say again is, what about his wife?"

"Oh I know, I know" Miss Paynton cried. "Yet why in the world should a thing go as far as that?"

"Yes, but won't it?"

"I can't help the gentleman falling in love with me, can I?"

"You needn't see him."

"Even when he doesn't know he is in love with me? Oh, I don't suppose he is. But Claire, he's all right. Takes me out of myself. I've told the poor man all about Terence, even a good deal about Campbell, and he's so truly sweet and understanding. I've actually been sleeping well, once again."

"There's worse things than lying awake."

"Oh Claire, darling" Miss Paynton called out in a bright delighted voice. "I knew you'd disapprove. You're out to make my poor flesh creep, is that it?"

"Well of course, Ann."

"I suppose we must be the only two close friends in the whole world could sit here, utterly different from one another, and still not agree, yet remain the closest of close to each other."

"But, my dear, I don't admit we are so very dissimilar" Miss Belaine objected.

"Why, how d'you mean?"

"Of course you're a hundred times prettier than me, naturally, yet I'd say quite likely we wanted the same things in the end, Ann."

"Without knowing what those were? Except the obvious ones, I mean?"

"Well, darling, now you are talking in riddles."

"In what way? I'm being flippant, is that it?"

"Not yet."

"I'm sorry Claire. You'll have to forgive. The truth is, all this I've been telling you will probably come to nothing, of course. And will end in tears probably, anyway. That's not the point. Oh dear, will you please look at the time. I must fly."

On which they kissed and left.

Arthur Middleton was giving Miss Paynton dinner in his flat. They were alone except for the cook who served them, and who was to go home as soon as she had washed up.

"Why didn't you say, when you asked me, that Diana and Peter weren't to be here?" Annabel demanded, a trace perhaps of severity in her tone.

"Didn't I?" Mr Middleton queried. "Possibly I forgot."

"I wouldn't think one could forget a little thing like that!"

"Really?" he enquired. "As a matter of fact, Peter gets most awfully hipped in London. After all there's not much for a boy here, is there? So Diana's taking him up for a spot of salmon fishing with her brother in Scotland."

"Oh dear" the girl said. "I could do with a bit of that myself."

"Yes, he is lucky, isn't he! But I didn't know that you cared about fishing, Ann?"

"I might if I ever had some" Miss Paynton answered. "Anything to get away from London, anyway."

"Why, aren't you happy here?"

"Who is?"

"What's the matter then?" he asked. "Your young men giving you trouble?"

"Oh I don't allow them to bother me" Miss Paynton replied with spirit. "No it's simply that you've been everywhere and I've never got even as far as Scotland, all my young life."

"Well in that case Ann, you must come up with us some time."

"Fat chance there is, I'd say."

"Why on earth not?"

"Peter's a bit young for me, you know" the girl propounded and gave Middleton a sad-seeming, long, low look.

"All right if you won't come with Peter you shall with us. One day" he added, virtuously.

"Oh I don't think so, no" she said and laughed.

"I thought you said you wanted to see Scotland."

"I did and I still do" the girl assured him.

"So we'd bore you?" he asked, with obvious petulance.

"Who's fishing for compliments now?" she demanded.

"What on earth do you mean by that, Ann?"

"You know perfectly well" she said. "There's no one in the whole wide world I'd rather go with than you" she averred "and darling Diana" she added, with a limpid look.

"Well then?"

"But you can't just cart me around as an extra daughter, can you?" Miss Paynton objected.

"It wouldn't be that sort of thing at all" he said.

"What else could it be then, Arthur?"

"What could it be?" he echoed. "D'you know what you're saying? As a matter of fact . . . Oh Lord . . . No, you're out to make difficulties, aren't you? If we wanted to take you along, we would because, because we wished."

"So I expect! But Arthur, how might it look?"

"Well there, I'm afraid, I can't follow" he said, with a hard note in his voice.

"Oh won't you understand there's nothing I'd like better, nothing" the girl insisted in a sort of wail. Upon which the cook came in with two grilled cutlets.

"No you simply shouldn't!" Miss Paynton protested. "Not your whole meat ration. Really it's too sweet!"

"Well they don't bother with regulations, up where Diana and Peter are going, so I thought we might just as well eat theirs this evening. Isn't that so, Mrs Everett?"

"Got to take what you can get these days" the cook replied and left.

"You are luxurious" the young lady said softly, to the closed door. "Mummy has to cook for all of us now their wages have gone up so terribly. It's awful not having even one servant sleeping on the premises. Mummy lives in terror of burglars when the house is left empty."

"We're in the same boat" Mr Middleton explained with what seemed to be elaborate unconcern. "When Mrs Everett packs up and goes home each evening, we're completely on our own. We've only dailies, too."

"But why didn't you say when you asked me?"

"Tell you what Ann?"

"That this was going to be like a Victorian melodrama. Me, all alone, with you, here!"

"Don't be so absurd, darling" he protested in a hard sort of voice. "You can't suppose, if you started screaming now, that someone like Mrs Everett would rush in to help."

"What?" Miss Paynton wailed.

"Nonsense, Ann. Of course she would. And I told Diana I'd asked you. In fact Diana ordered the meal herself."

"Oh I was just only thinking of Mummy" the girl said in a petulant, dissatisfied tone of voice.

"Then if Paula's got any complaints she can take them to Mrs Middleton" the man said drily.

"Now you are really going all Victorian" Miss Paynton cried, and laughed in almost a wanton fashion.

"How so?" he demanded.

"Why, when you talk of darling Diana with that absurdly formal voice."

"I like to show respect where respect is due" the husband objected.

"I know" Miss Paynton said, with a sad smile.

"What do you know?"

"If I told, Arthur, you'd only say I was trying flattery."

"I can't find out, my dear, until you consent to put whatever it is, into words." In his turn he smiled gloomily at the girl.

"It's so difficult to express" she at once informed the man. "Something people my age simply don't seem to have for one another. Respect" she ended.

"The only way to gain that, is to live with another person long enough."

"What an extraordinary idea, darling" and she gave a disagreeable sort of laugh.

"Why?" he demanded.

"D'you honestly mean you would have to live with me for years before you could ever bring yourself to respect me."

"Oh I wasn't being personal, Ann."

"I might have known you wouldn't be, where I was concerned" she said in a most petulant voice.

"Here" he protested. "Steady on! How could I have given you that idea?"

"I know what you meant" she insisted.

"If I've been very tiresome, well then I apologise" Mr Middleton announced with a small smile.

"Oh you haven't! It's all in me . . . in me" she wailed at once.

"I always seem to produce this effect" he went on, still smiling as if to apologise.

"Oh, do you?" she asked. "That makes everything much better." She smiled mischievously at him now. "Then it isn't just only me! Tell about the others you have here" she continued. "How do they put up with it?"

"Don't be absurd, Ann" he protested. "How often, after all, does Diana go away?"

"How should I know?" she countered. "But do you have to get a girl alone then, do you, to have that effect on her?"

"It wouldn't be very amusing for Diana if I entertained girls here with her."

"So you don't have 'girls' as you call them to dinner every night" she said, it seemed almost in triumph.

"Of course not, Ann."

"Then what did you mean when you said you always had that certain effect on the poor dears?"

"I suppose it was just a figure of speech" he said.

"I bet" she crowed. Her face was now alight with what was obviously amusement. "Because it's only right that I should be very interested in marriage" she went on. "Tell me, what does happen?"

"In marriage? Pretty well everything you can imagine."

"No, now don't be disgusting" she demanded with a straight face. "I'm not like you, I really intend all I say. What I want to know is, can you take out the people you want, separately I mean."

"Diana and I never felt we should sit down and mope when chance left either of us on our own."

"So you're just not sitting down and moping now?"

"Exactly."

She laughed a gay laugh, and looked at him.

"And you?" he smiled back.

"Oh me?" she replied, instantly serious. "Why, you're simply saving my life!"

"Now Annabel!" he protested. "What is this?"

"But it's true" she insisted. "You can't imagine what things can be like when one goes out with Campbell!"

"Who can't?" Mr Middleton demanded. "I can."

"So you're just going to be nasty" she pouted. "No, he talks of himself, nearly all the time. And he's so depressed, poor sweet! It's not that I don't love him, I do, I dote on him, but he's a rainmaker, stay with Campbell a couple of hours and heavy clouds at once begin to gather."

"That doesn't sound very gay."

"My dear, it isn't" she said, rather glum.

"Well, shall we have our ice now?" he asked, and rang. "I'm afraid there's nothing more. Hasn't been much for you, has there, worse luck."

"Oh Mrs Everett" Miss Paynton cried, as this lady immediately came in "I've had such a delicious dinner. And now an ice! No, it's too much!"

"Not enough to keep my old parrot pecking" the cook drily replied, without a glance, and left again.

Arthur Middleton went to the door.

"Mrs Everett" he called "we'll have our coffee in the sitting room." Then he shut the door and sat down.

"I can't imagine why Diana ordered ices" he complained. "She knows very well my teeth are too shaky to eat them."

"You ought to go to a dentist then."

"That's just it, Annabel. You were asking a moment ago about marriage. Well, it consists in one's having teeth too uncertain for certain foods and no attention paid at all, none in the least! In fact one seems to get those dishes all the more often."

"Poor you."

"I say, Ann, that's a very attractive dress you've got on this evening!"

"D'you really think so?"

"I do."

"You don't think it's too low?" she asked in a matter of fact voice.

"Why not at all" he protested. "Besides, it lets one see your shoulders."

"All the same I daren't hardly laugh in it" she said and giggled.

"Go on, try" he encouraged, with a sort of fixed grin.

"Now that's not nice" she reproved Mr Middleton.

"You have the most lovely shoulders, Ann."

"I do! You promise?"

"Yes."

"Oh how nice! And what very good ices your Mrs Everett makes."

"They come from round the corner."

"They can't!"

"You can buy eatable ices anywhere over the way, but one doesn't come across someone like you in a month of Sundays."

"I don't think that's very flattering" she objected in a bored voice.

"Well then, now you've finished, shall we go and have coffee Ann?"

"Yes, let's" she said, rising to lead a way into the next room.

Here they found a deep sofa drawn up to face the fire.

"Arthur" she almost accused him "you've been pulling the furniture about. I don't remember this, here, before."

"I felt it was rather cold tonight. So I moved everything out from that bookcase because I thought we'd be more cosy."

"I see" she said and sat down on it.

"What d'you have, white or black?"

"Oh black please. Don't you remember?"

The tray with their coffee things stood on rather a high trolley. When he had served Miss Paynton and sat down at her side, the pot stood almost at the level of his eyes.

"I've never been out to dinner alone with you before" he excused himself. "I know you take white at lunch, of course." He gulped his down at one go.

The young lady sipped hers. "You give one such a lot to drink" she announced.

"Nonsense" he said and then they both fell silent.

But when she had drained her cup, she reached up to put this away on the trolley and as she leant back once more it was to find that he had put an arm along the back of the sofa and that she was, so to speak, sitting against it. His hand closed on the bare shoulder. Without looking at him she reached her far hand over and put it over his. Then, when she felt him pulling at her she said "Arthur" expressionlessly, and half turned her head away.

He was seated beside the girl but rather too far off. Also this trolley, between the two of them and that fire, was hard by his knees. It seemed he could not move over easily. So he went on pulling, and, as she tilted towards him, he put his far hand round her chin to turn this in his direction. She quietly rubbed this chin against his palm. Then she gently subsided on the man's shoulder.

They kissed.

"Darling" he murmured. "So beautiful. Delicious."

"Oh Arthur" she said in just that expiring sigh she used to bring telephone conversations to an end.

They kissed again.

Then, probably because he was uncomfortable, for by the looks of it he had too far to reach to get at her, he dropped the far hand under her legs to lift these over his knees. He drew them unresisting to him, but must have forgotten the trolley. For the slow sweep he was imposing on her legs engaged her feet with that trolley and the coffee pot came over onto both.

"My dress!" she exclaimed in a loud, despairing voice.

"Damn" he said.

The girl at once jumped to her feet. The trolley almost went into the fire and that coffee pot rolled off their laps onto the floor.

"Hot boiling water" she cried out.

"Oh God, and to think Mrs Everett's gone home" he yelled.

They started together, fast, for the passage. Once outside, he shouted "in here" throwing open his and Diana's bedroom. There was a bathroom opened out of this, but, because the space was small, a basin with hot and cold water had been fitted by Diana's bed. It was to this that Miss Paynton ran. Turning the hot tap on, she zipped off her skirt, and stood with her fat legs starting out of lace knickers.

"Here, let me" he said, and knelt at her side.

She picked the handkerchief out of his breast pocket, drenched it in that basin, and then, putting her hand inside the skirt she had discarded, she began to rub at the stain.

And it was at this moment Diana entered.

She stood at the door with a completely expressionless face.

"Arthur" she said "when you've done, could you come outside a minute."

After one scared glance, Annabel went on rubbing.

Mr Middleton left the bedroom immediately, closing the door behind him.

"What on earth do you think you are doing?" she demanded of her husband in a low voice, then went on. "It's about Peter" and she seemed to choke. "A taxi smash. He's in hospital, Arthur! On the way to that beastly train!"

"Hospital? Taxi smash? Why didn't you tell me?"

"We never caught it, you see. Oh, he's all right. But, poor sweet, he was unconscious. I thought why bother you when the doctors said he was in no danger – before the X-ray. Though if I'd known how you were behaving – I must say!" All this Diana said in a level, hurried voice.

Then she slowed down. "Now they've seen the prints, nothing's cracked and he's conscious again. Oh my dear!"

"Peter?" he stammered. "On the way to the station? But why didn't you tell me?"

"Would it have made any difference?" she replied. "Though he has an awful head, now" she added with a smile. "The poor darling!"

"Well what are we waiting for?" he demanded. "Let's get to him!"

"And how about that little bitch in there?" Mrs Middleton asked, in the same level tones.

"She's just getting a coffee stain from off her dress" her husband told her.

"Quite so, Arthur, but I saw your hand."

"Damn my hand. Now about Peter . . . "

"I saw your hand" she repeated in an awful voice.

"What about my hand, don't be so childish . . . ?"

"We won't discuss this any more, if you please" she calmly interrupted him.

"I wasn't doing nothing" he protested.

"Never mind about that now." His wife raised her voice. "Are you going to stand here all night with your son in hospital?" Then she added, most severely "I saw you."

"Oh God!" he cried.

He opened that bedroom door a crack so he could not see the girl inside, and announced "Oh Annabel, Peter's been in an accident but he's quite all right, and we're off to the hospital." To this he got no reply. He shut the door. "Come on!" his wife insisted with great impatience, and they hastened off together.

Mr Middleton, next morning, did no business at all before he had persuaded his friend Addinsell to throw over a previous engagement to lunch.

"I'm in trouble, Charles" he said.

"How's that?"

"Well Diana was taking Peter in a taxi to catch the train for Scotland when they had a smash and Peter was knocked out. The boy's all right now, though, no bones broken, or even a fractured skull as we feared at first."

"I say, I am sorry. What a rotten thing to happen!"

"Yes, and that's not the whole of it, as a matter of fact. To tell the honest truth, I'm in a spot of bother with Diana, Charles."

"How so?"

"Well, of course, all my silly fault" Mr Middleton explained. "I'd asked this Paynton girl alone to dinner." At this point Mr Addinsell laughed. "Don't do that" Arthur Middleton exclaimed. "I told Diana; in fact she ordered the meal. But what happened was a stupid accident." Here he paused.

"Your wife came back to find you tucked up in bed together" the other man suggested.

"For God's sake don't be so foul" Mr Middleton appealed. "There was nothing of that sort. No, we had a slight accident. Ann spilled some coffee over her dress. God, I don't like to think of it, even now!"

Again he paused.

"And so what?" Addinsell demanded.

"And so Charles, Diana came in while Ann was dealing with this stain I told you about."

"Well come on, Arthur."

"As a matter of fact, Ann had whipped her skirt off" Arthur Middleton explained in a peculiarly shamefaced way.

"You old devil!" his companion commented.

"Oh there was nothing of that sort" the husband protested. "Well, to be truthful, I won't pretend there mightn't have been, but only, so to say, thirty minutes later. If you know what I mean. No all this was as innocent as the day, at the time I'm talking of. Then here's Diana all at once in the room when she should by rights have been steaming past Rugby at sixty miles an hour and so upset about Peter, as was only natural . . ."

"Did she herself get hurt, at all?"

"In the smash? No, thank heavens. But she decidedly cut up rough over Ann's skirt being off."

"Not to be wondered at, Arthur, really."

"No, I know, and in her own bedroom, too. Yet Charles, I've never been a jealous husband. Even my worst enemy would grant me that."

"So if you came back unexpectedly" Mr Addinsell opposed "you'd ignore her dinner guest who'd happened to find himself without his trousers."

"Well I don't know about overlooking it, but surely to goodness I wouldn't make the scene Diana made!"

"You forget she was naturally upset about Peter."

"That's what I told her this morning, Charles, when we went into the whole thing again."

"And what did she say?"

"She wouldn't bite."

"Great mistake to hold inquests, Arthur. Greatest mistake there is, in life."

"You wait until you're married again! You'll find you have no choice."

"All right, all right" Mr Addinsell admitted. "Well, what do you want me to do?"

"You see, I've a dinner to the general managers Tuesday" Mr Middleton said, almost in the voice of a conspirator. "And I was wondering if, for old sake's sake, for my sake, you'd ask Diana out to dinner that evening. With any luck she won't discuss it. But if she does, just remind her, will you, old man, there's never been anyone else in my whole life, really! You know that! You know me almost as well as I do . . . "

"O.K." Mr Addinsell said, "I'll try. Though it's a bit of a tall order!"

Later that same afternoon, when he got back to the office, he was just in time to take a call from Miss Paynton.

"Oh Arthur" she sighed, in her signing-off voice.

"Peter's absolutely all right" he said quickly. "Of course he's got a stupendous headache, but there's nothing broken, and they're even getting him up tomorrow."

"Splendid" she said with a doleful tone.

"Yes, isn't it" he hesitantly agreed.

"And darling Diana?" she breathed.

"There's been a spot of bother, there" he admitted. "In fact I'm in bad odour for the moment. But it was mainly the shock. She was in the taxi too, you know. She escaped by bracing herself back on the seat."

"It's too awful" Miss Paynton exclaimed, with a firmer voice. "One never knows where one's safe these days."

"Yes" he admitted.

"And is she still very cross with you?" she enquired.

"Yes" he said. "And with you a bit, too, as a matter of fact."

"Me?" she fluted. "But why ever over me?"

"Well, of course, she'd just been in rather a nasty smash" Arthur Middleton explained. "Poor darling. And she was worried stiff about Peter."

He paused.

"Arthur!" Miss Paynton said. "D'you think I could see you for say five minutes, after work. I'm fussed."

He did not answer at once. "Well" he at last replied. "I'm not sure that would be an altogether good notion, Ann. Just at the moment" he added.

71

"I see" she said.

A click then told him she had rung off.

Mrs Middleton was having her third conversation with her husband on the subject of Annabel Paynton. The attitude she adopted appeared to be one of pained surprise, of grieving bewilderment.

"No, Arthur, I shall never understand" she said. "Just when Peter was lain like dead in the ambulance and there was I imagining him gone."

"You're not to give this another thought" he murmured in a reassuring voice.

"But I can't help myself, Arthur!"

"Now, my dear, you'll make yourself ill if you go on visualising Peter unconscious."

"I'm not" she objected, as if to a child. "Arthur, I saw your hand!"

"My darling, we've been into this so often" he implored. "To my last breath I'll always maintain I'd done nothing with my hand."

"I saw."

"Then, come on now, which hand was it?"

"What difference does that make?"

"Tell me, Diana" he begged. "The left or the right?"

"Oh no" she broke out "this is too brutal. Why must you torture me so?"

"I didn't bring the subject up, darling."

"But you see" she said, her eyes very wide "I smelled you, Arthur!"

"You smelt me? This is something new! And what d'you mean by that?"

"Why the powder she had on, or the scent she used, Arthur!"

"Now my dear, which? You know you've always prided yourself on your sense of smell. If this is right, what you're saying, you ought to be able to tell one from the other."

"Don't try and dodge" she informed him in the same sad voice. "I did, I tell you."

"I can't make this out at all. What am I supposed to have done now?"

"You'd put your hand on her leg, Arthur, and I can't, I shan't, ever, get over it."

"Look darling" he said, most reasonably. "Will you believe me when I say I have absolutely no recollection of anything of the kind."

"Are you trying to tell me, then, that you didn't?"

"Well, really, I'd say I might remember a little thing like that!"

"But Arthur, I smelled you!"

"Oh damn this famous sense of smell of yours" he exclaimed with warmth.

"I can't help it, can I" she suggested, in a voice of resignation. "I was born that way."

"Look darling" he said and seemed to whip himself almost into a sense of eagerness "be reasonable about this, don't let's get carried away. You can't call to mind which hand of mine it was, and you don't know what I'm supposed to have smelt of."

"Why, of that horrible little Annabel, of course, Arthur!"

"Now darling" he said again "let's just face things. Coffee does get spilt you know."

"Yes, but how? You've never even once told me."

"Oh, in the way coffee always does get spilt."

"There must have been something happened to make it, Arthur."

"Well, you see, darling, I'd drawn the sofa out across the fire . . . "

"Yes, and what for, thank you?"

"I simply thought we'd be more cosy; then . . . "

"You're never to turn the furniture round again" she raised her voice at last. "It's my house . . . "

"I live here too," he broke in.

"I'm in all the time" she expostulated.

"So I only wish you could have been present, Di, and seen with your own eyes how truly innocent the whole thing was."

"D'you suppose I wanted to be at that awful hospital?" she demanded in a calmer voice.

"Good heavens no, darling! No, in getting my coffee I stupidly, clumsy fool that I am, just jogged her elbow."

"Well then?"

"Well then, I don't suppose she has much of a dress allowance, if there is still such a thing these days, and she called out, 'hot boiling water' was the phrase she used, and of course I lost my head and rushed her into our bedroom, meaning to get her in the bath."

Mrs Middleton at this moment let out a laugh in which there was very little fun.

"Well, as a matter of fact, she may have been first, before me" Mr Middleton corrected himself. "Because once Ann had seen the basin she wouldn't go any further, she peeled off her skirt at once."

"But, Arthur, what could have made you kneel?"

"My dear, can't you see? I was in an agony of embarrassment."

"Not at her fat legs, I don't suppose?"

"Now look here, my dear, there's no need to be insulting, is there? How d'you suppose it would look, to Paula, if at my age I bought her girl a new dress."

"There are such things as cleaners and I've got clothes" his wife told him in an expressionless voice.

"Then I give up" he said wearily. "All I did was for the best, darling. I seem to have made a complete ass of myself and there it is."

"She did of you, you mean" Mrs Middleton corrected him. "Well darling" she added with a tired smile "don't bother your old head too much. You see, I love you. There . . . "

He came over. They kissed as though they had been parted a long time.

"I do love you" she repeated. "And I've been upset. But don't let me ever catch you, even once, again . . . "

"Now darling!" he protested.

"All right, we won't talk of it just now" she ended. She then told him Addinsell had asked her out to dinner. When he expressed a sort of resigned pleasure, they animatedly discussed Peter's splendid progress out of his concussion.

"What's the matter with Arthur these days?" Mr Addinsell asked Diana as he drove her away for the dinner they were to have together. "Lately he's seemed a different fellow."

Mrs Middleton laughed selfconsciously. "I'm afraid I may have been a bit difficult the last few days."

"In what way, may one ask?"

"Well, there was that terrible accident Peter and I were involved in. You see, Peter has been kept in hospital with a bit of concussion, but we are getting him back tomorrow, so things are looking up again."

"Yes, I was sorry to hear. Is Peter going to be all right?"

"Oh absolutely! The doctors are delighted. But of course, as you can imagine, Charles, I didn't know, not at first. In fact, I nearly worried myself out of my poor mind."

Mr Addinsell had to draw up rather suddenly at some traffic lights. She put her hands against the dashboard.

"Oh, do be careful" she cried, then seemed to recover herself. "I'm terribly sorry. But I've been nervous ever since we were in that awful smash."

"Only natural!" he said.

"Yes I'm afraid I've made myself such a bore to Arthur the last day or two" she went on in a nervous voice. "Of course he can be maddening sometimes, who isn't, ever, in married life? And I only say this to you because you are Arthur's oldest friend."

"Go on" he said when she paused.

"Well, maddening is not quite the word I should have used, perhaps. But, Charles, although it's natural, after so many years of being married, it is sad, isn't it, when the man begins to look elsewhere?"

"Old Arthur? My dear, I can assure you . . . "

"No Charles" she said "I've had proof. And I never intended to say a word of all this. So dull for you!"

"Why!" he exclaimed, and drove with great caution. "You two are my greatest friends. Nothing dull where you're both concerned."

"You are sweet, Charles. Still, this is not a topic to go out to dinner on, is it? Let's talk about you, for a change. Why did you never marry again?"

Mr Addinsell accelerated past a taxi.

"I honestly don't know" he replied. "Never found anyone who would have me, I suppose."

"Now that's just not true. It can't be! But there are times I lie awake, Charles, and wonder, and think how terribly wise you've been."

"Me?" he asked, with what seemed to be genuine amazement. "My dear I seem to have done nothing but lose money all my life."

"No, don't joke about this" she reproved him. "Just think of it all. There are the children. Sometimes I thank Providence we've only one. They get ill, they nearly die and you're almost out of your mind, Peter has this terrible affair, and, the whole while, your husband is getting tired of you."

"Now Diana . . . "

"I know" she interrupted "but that's only natural, isn't it? This is the way things are, Charles!"

"I'm sure Arthur . . . "

"And we can't change them" she insisted. "There are moments I feel it would be almost presumptuous to try. One has to learn one can't go against the laws of nature, and that can be a very painful experience, as I've just discovered, to my cost."

"My dear" he asked "what is this?"

"He's found another girl" she told him in a very small voice.

"But that's preposterous" Mr Addinsell began, when she cut in with,

"Oh damn, I think I'm going to cry."

Upon which he drew in to the side of the road, put his arm round her shoulder. While she turned her face away, he demanded, "Now Diana what is all this?"

She held her breath while two tears came down each side of her nose. She did not answer.

"There are days I wonder" he said in low tones "if we aren't, every one of us, at our lowest, this time of the year." He looked to his front, the windscreen wiper clicked and hissed to and fro. "Wet streets, rainclouds down to the tops of the houses, this awful damp, and if you get a cold you can't seem to throw it off, there's nothing worse than our English winter" he concluded.

She blew her nose, seemed to get herself under control. Then he put his far hand over, under her chin, turned this towards him and gently kissed her wet mouth. She as quietly responded.

"I'm sorry I'm such a fool" she said.

"You weren't" he replied. "Now we'd better get under way, again, before a policeman catches up."

"Drive slowly, won't you" she begged. "While I repair the damage." She got out her bag.

"Of course, and don't talk of what's bothering you, unless you want."

She spoke in a smothered sort of voice from under her powder puff.

"I swore I wouldn't, but now I can't seem to help myself" she said.

"Then come out with it" he encouraged.

"Only that I came home and found him in bed with that horrible little Annabel Paynton" she lied.

"It's not possible, my dear!" Mr Addinsell protested, in a shocked voice.

"Oh yes, and stark naked, of course. Oh whatever am I to say to Paula, if she should get to learn?"

"I can't believe it" Arthur's best friend said. "The silly juggins!"

"And I, who'd come back to tell him his own son was unconscious in hospital!"

"Didn't they say anything?"

"What was there to tell me?"

"No, quite. But he made out to me she'd spilt some coffee on her dress."

"So he's spoken to you?" she said, still working on her face. "Oh I expect they began like that, but it's how this thing ended" she lied and did not look at Addinsell. "You won't mention this to a soul, of course?"

"Me?" he asked. "Rather cut my tongue off first!"

"So now I've told you" she exclaimed. She put away her bag again. "You're a great comfort, Charles" she said and put her hand rather heavily on his arm. The car swerved. "Oh" she cried. "Oh Charles. I'm so sorry" she added "all my own hysterical, silly fault!"

"That's all right" he reassured her. "No harm done at all."

"Ah, but there might have been" she responded. "That's the way tragedies happen."

"So how did all this end between you and Arthur?"

"Does anything ever end?" she objected. "I called him out, of course. I had to tell him about Peter. Then I went back to the hospital and didn't show a thing to the boy, I can at least say that for myself."

"Good for you Diana!"

"Now we must be somewhere near the restaurant you are taking me to and I absolutely refuse to talk about myself any more, or to allow you to."

And she kept him to this. Once or twice in the evening she made him swear again he would not tell a soul, but, beyond that, she would not let him refer to what she said she had seen.

When he drove her back home she permitted him to stop the car a little distance from her door and kiss her quite hard. She cried a bit again, then, but said no more before she left him.

The next day, when Peter was discharged from hospital, his parents received the young man almost as though he were back from the dead.

"Well, my dear boy" the father cried aloud "this really is something!" and shook him by the hand.

"But how are you, darling?" Diana insisted.

"Bloody awful" the boy said.

"Sit down at once. Now tell me, quite calmly, are you still in pain?"

"God yes" the young man answered. "And the nights are agony."

"Really Arthur!" the wife, his mother, broke out in ringing tones "have they any right to let patients out in his condition?"

"I suppose they need the beds" Mr Middleton remarked in what was, probably, too casual a tone.

"Then they are murderers" she said with firmness. "Arthur, should he go to a nursing home, d'you think?"

"Now, hang on a minute" the boy protested. "It's death in those places, they nearly kill you. You can't want to send me in again?"

"But you don't seem well at all, to me, darling."

"Oh I suppose I've what they call recovered" her son admitted with obvious reluctance. "But, d'you know, three people died in my ward, while I was there?"

"Don't, darling" said his mother.

"I really think you might have put me in a private room."

"Where was the money to come from?" his father asked.

"There you go again, Arthur" Mrs Middleton complained. "When Peter's all we have!" Then, in a sinister voice, she added "Now!"

"Thirty guineas a week?" the husband queried.

"Three days" she answered. "And how much in that time do you spend on gin?"

"Oh come, Diana darling, you like your glass as well."

"I need it" she replied, emphatically.

"Yes, at least three people died" Peter interjected.

"No, don't" was Mrs Middleton's earnest plea.

"What time of the day or night?" his father wanted to be told.

"Usually it seemed to be about four or five in the morning."

"But weren't you asleep then?"

"God, you don't sleep in those places."

"Curious" Mr Middleton remarked "it always seems that resistance is lowest at that hour of the night."

"And this time of year" his wife murmured.

"You wouldn't joke about it if you'd just seen three people die before your very eyes!"

"I wasn't joking, Peter" Mr Middleton explained.

"What I can't make out" the boy went on "is why, at my age, you send me to a place like that."

"Because I thought you'd been killed" his mother told him in a great voice. "I had to get you somewhere at once" she added.

"Well, it was absolute hell" the boy said.

"But are you all right now?" Mr Middleton demanded.

"Yes, fairly."

"Does it hurt you still?"

"Of course."

"Then are you enough all right to go up with your mother to Uncle Dick's?"

"Oh I'd still like to get in some fishing."

"It's so dull for him in the holidays, this time of the year, Arthur."

"Don't I know" the man exclaimed, almost with vexation. "But it would be unfair on your brother to send the boy up to him if he was going to be ill, even if you were there to nurse him."

"But, darling Peter, you'd get along all right without me?"

"Aren't you going now, then?" her husband demanded.

"Well naturally I'll travel if Peter needs me" the mother promised. "Surely, darling, you'll get along all right, alone with Uncle Dick?"

"Why, don't you want to come up with me?"

"You see, my dear, I've had really rather a shock!"

"You were hurt in the smash?" her son asked her, with what seemed to be distaste.

"Well, perhaps" she said, looking hard at the husband.

"And are you all right now?" the boy enquired.

"Yes and no" she answered.

After which it was agreed they should get their doctor's opinion on Peter's travelling. When this turned out to be favourable he journeyed up alone next day.

On the Monday Mr Middleton rang Ann Paynton. She blandly agreed to meet him that morning, at the usual time and place, for lunch.

She was first, and, when she shook him by the hand, "I thought I was never going to see you again" she said.

"Oh now, hardly as bad as that" he answered.

She laughed. "I don't know, Arthur. At the time I thought things were pretty fierce."

He simpered. "Nice of you to make a joke, Ann."

"Though it wasn't very funny, then, after all" she countered, in what appeared to be disgust.

"Perfectly appalling for both of us" he agreed.

"Oh, Arthur, I do so want to apologise" she nervously said. "I can't think what came over me to take off my skirt, except of course, panic."

"And if I hadn't been such a damn fool to spill coffee all over you, as though I, at my age, didn't know how to kiss a girl, then none of this would have happened!"

"Don't let's talk of that" she implored, examining her shoes. "But I have so few clothes. My one idea was to get the stain out. Honest!"

"Yes Ann, I know" Mr Middleton earnestly agreed.

"So there was trouble?"

"Yes."

"Bad trouble, Arthur?"

"Pretty bad."

"Oh dear. I think perhaps you'd better give me a drink."

They went to the bar. After a moment or two she giggled.

"What's that for?" he asked.

"Your face" she replied.

"What's wrong with it?" He twisted until he could see himself in a mirror.

"Not now" she giggled. "Then."

Mr Middleton looked ruefully at himself. "When I was down on my knees?" he queried, watching his own reflection.

"Oh yes" she said, in plain delight.

He turned back to the girl.

"Diana's been giving me some of that" he told her.

"Oh you poor dear" Miss Paynton cried and patted his knee as he sat beside her, up at the bar. "What do I want to bring that up for, just when you have at last asked me out again? So Peter's all right?"

"Yes, thank God."

"And they're both off to Scotland?"

"No. Diana wouldn't go."

"Is it serious then, Arthur? About Diana I mean?"

"I don't know" he said. "I can't make out."

"Why, whatever's happened?"

"Well, we've been married eighteen years, Ann, and I've never known anything like this, ever."

"Like what?"

"It's hard to describe. You see, I love my wife" he announced in a low voice, with unction. "We've always trusted one another. Now, all on one side, that seems to have evaporated, and in a night!"

The young lady said nothing. She watched him.

"I don't know whether it wouldn't be a good idea if you went to her and explained, Ann." He did not look at Miss Paynton as he suggested this.

"I'd not be too keen" she replied, still closely watching the man.

"D'you think?" he murmured.

"Mightn't work out at all" she said.

"Oh well, if you feel that way, Ann."

"D'you mind?"

"No, it was just a thought. But I don't fancy the idea of Diana going to Paula."

"To Mummy?" the girl cried. "Oh things are really serious, then!" she wailed. "Why she couldn't! That would be really the end!"

"I mean if you could somehow apologise?"

"But what for?" Miss Paynton demanded with spirit. "For being kissed by a person who then went and upset all the coffee over my dress? Oh Lord, now I shall really have to tell Mummy."

"Now for heaven's sake, Ann, don't you go to Paula with this!" She bit her pretty lip.

"I must get in first" she explained.

"But listen, you can . . . "

"Has Diana actually said she was going?" the daughter interrupted.

"Not yet."

"Oh, it's a disaster" Miss Paynton exclaimed, with extreme symptoms of disquiet, although she kept her voice down, and only an acute observer of this scene could have noticed the untoward. "Then my whole reputation's at stake?"

"But this was all an accident, Ann."

"Fat lot of difference that will make when Mummy hears" the girl said, with what might be described as indignation.

"But has she actually said she was to go to Mummy?"

"No."

"At the same time you think she will?"

"Not really."

"Now look, Arthur. This could be vital to me. Is she, or isn't she? If you've been married for eighteen years you ought to know! Will she go or not?"

"Probably not."

"That's no great comfort" the young lady objected.

"I'm sorry I started this" Mr Middleton proclaimed. "Diana never said she had that in mind, even. I expect I have too vivid an imagination. I just wondered if it mightn't be a good idea if you dropped in to see Di."

"Has the same sort of happening happened before?"

"Ann, what is this?"

"Has she been to anyone else's mother?"

"No, of course not."

"Then I'll tell you what. I won't go to Mummy if you swear, swear mind, you'll let me know in good time beforehand if she actually threatens to."

"But of course, Ann. What d'you take me for?"

"I'm sorry. I got upset."

"It's I who ought to apologise" he said with an air of considerable relief. "When all's said and done, I started this."

"Then what made you imagine Diana was going to?"

"She's been in such a curious way lately" he replied.

"How?"

"Well, by not travelling with Peter to Scotland, for one."

"I expect she may wish to keep an eye on you, Arthur, just over the next week or two."

"I'm not sure of that" he said. "And there's this whole business of Charles Addinsell."

"I don't know about him, do I?"

"Old friend of ours, Ann. But, dammit, she's been out with Charles three times in five whole days."

"You mean he's a flame?"

"Of course not, Ann. Don't be ridiculous, if you'll excuse the expression. As a matter of fact he's a very old friend of mine and I asked him myself, when this happened, to take her out."

"Well then! Everything's perfect, isn't it?"

"That's exactly what I don't know."

"Arthur!" she demanded. "Are you, yourself, jealous now?"

"I don't know" he dully repeated.

"You are!" she insisted.

"And if I am, why shouldn't I be?" he asked, with some signs of irritation.

"Yet she hasn't been caught with her skirt off too, has she?"

"Really, Ann" he protested. "You go too far!"

"I'm sorry, truly I am" she replied with a show of great conviction. "But what makes you think, then, the way you do?"

"Well, you know, three times in five days! When they'd hardly before been out together more than once a week! What d'you suppose they're saying all those hours?"

"I've simply no idea" she answered, with a straight face.

Then their barman asked if they had any further orders and they realised that lunch must be almost over. Hurrying into the restaurant, they ate in haste and did not again refer to Mrs Middleton. In fact they cheered up, teased each other, and became quite gay on lager beer.

The next evening Mr Addinsell was driving Diana Middleton home after he had given her dinner.

"Come up to my rooms and have one for the road" he suggested in a casual sort of voice. "Before I drop you back."

"Oh I've had so much to drink already, Charles" she said and giggled.

"Nonsense, Di. Do you good. Only just round this corner here."

"Well then, if it's only the one" she agreed. She yawned. "You're such a help to me" she added.

"Got to get out of oneself, every once and again" he said. "And, you know, you're a very, very attractive woman."

"Now Charles" she reproved with a kind of lazy indulgence. "If we have any more of that, I'll take a taxi off the nearest rank. Besides, you don't begin to mean it."

"Have things your own way. Here we are" he announced, drawing up.

Upstairs, as he poured gin into her glass, she called out,

"Stop! That's quite enough. D'you want to make me drunk?"

They sat side by side on a sofa. He took her hand. After squeezing his once, she removed hers.

"Let's be serious a moment" she suggested. "I've been awfully good this whole evening, haven't I? Never even mentioned Arthur and my wretched affairs a single time. But just tell me this one thing. D'you think I should tell Paula?"

"Paula Paynton? What for?"

"Well, to warn her!"

"Would that help?"

"But Charles, in fairness to herself she ought to know her daughter's going to bed with men old enough to be the little creature's father."

"If you do that" he objected "you'll have Prior Paynton round to horsewhip Arthur."

She gave a delighted laugh.

"Oh I don't think so, Charles! Prior's not that sort of man at all."

He took a gulp at his gin.

"Can't be too careful. Could make quite a lot of talk" he said.

"Yes, I expect there might be a bit of a sensation. I see what you mean" she conceded.

"I'm thinking of you" he told Diana Middleton, and put his nearest arm around her shoulders. She laid the glass down.

"Oh Charles!" she said, in a grateful voice.

They kissed for quite a time. Then she drew away, and he allowed this.

"I simply must come up for air" she announced. "Oh Lord, how can I look?"

"Lovely as always" he answered, drawing her into another kiss. This time she withdrew after only a moment.

"You do more than something to me, Charles" she said, in what seemed to be wonder.

He put his mouth close to her ear.

"Let's go upstairs" he suggested, in a flat voice.

"But, my dear" she objected "you're all on the one floor in this place!"

"Next door" he levelly corrected.

She pecked a kiss at him.

"No, Charles. Two wrongs don't make a right, do they?"

Mr Addinsell relaxed his hold.

"Bother Arthur!" he complained.

"Oh don't I know, darling! Oh Charles, you are sweet, but can't you see it wouldn't be right?"

"This is just the two of us" he argued.

She briefly kissed the man once more.

"I'll say so" she conceded. "And then, no, Charles! You are one of the few people in the world I'd do it with, and yet I can't! You see that, don't you?"

"Suppose I must."

"And you won't be terribly cross?"

"Whatever you say, Di."

"Not exasperated, or anything?"

"No."

"Then, Charles, kiss me once again, because I have to go."

They kissed.

"I'll run you back" he announced as, without lingering, he rose from the sofa.

"Even after I've behaved like this? Now you are truly being noble" she said, on which they left.

Nothing else of consequence passed that night between them.

The next afternoon Miss Paynton met her confidante in the pub, after work. They drank light ale.

"The plot thickens" Annabel announced.

"I thought it might."

"I was caught by his wife with my skirt off whilst he knelt at my feet." This account was met in silence. Miss Paynton then let out a sort of scared giggle.

"Well, go on, Ann. There must be more."

"Oh he ran! She'd come back unexpectedly to fetch him. When she burst in on us she called him out and they both went off without another word to me."

"And have you seen the chap since?"

"Of course."

"Ann, you are a perfect idiot! What were the repercussions?"

"Fairly severe, I fancy" Miss Paynton replied in a satisfied kind of voice.

"Look out that nothing boomerangs back on your head, then."

"But how d'you mean? I couldn't help his spilling coffee over my dress, could I?"

"Well, anyone could dodge being caught."

"What can you mean, Claire?"

"Why actually take the skirt off, Ann, in where you were?"

"Because it was fairly on the way to being ruined. His maid was gone. We were alone. There wasn't even a kettle on. What else could I do?"

"Not be found there with him" Miss Belaine proposed.

"If you think I went to his flat for a purpose, then you're very much mistaken, Claire."

"Well, for the matter of that, why did you go?"

"You say I oughtn't so much as go out to lunch in public with Arthur? Because one thing leads to another? Is that it?"

"You're being promiscuous, Ann."

"I'm not!" Miss Paynton protested in ringing, confident tones. "I only know Campbell and a schoolboy, and how am I to meet anyone if I don't show myself."

"Yet just because you do go out to restaurants with Mr Middleton for lunch, here you are having to come back to his flat alone after dinner."

"I'd only been the once."

"Yet you'll find yourself there again, if he asks you?"

"I don't think he will, not now" Miss Paynton said. She giggled.

"And what does go on when you're with him?"

"We talk" the girl said, it seemed with satisfaction. "Mostly about his boy, Peter. You see I'm so much nearer to Peter in age than his father is. And he simply dotes on him. Of course he kisses me every now and again."

"Does he?"

"All right, when you go out, doesn't your Percival kiss you."

"I suppose so. Then he isn't married!"

"But this is just like a Victorian melodrama, once more" Miss Paynton exclaimed. "What's a kiss between friends, good heavens?"

"And supposing his wife tells your mother?"

"She couldn't!"

"She might."

"Why? What for?"

"'Hell hath no fury like a woman scorned'" Miss Belaine quoted.

"But she hasn't even been scorned, Claire."

"Why not?"

"He dotes on her! I must have told you. He honestly does."

"Well, he may. But being the person he obviously is, Ann, don't you think she may end up scorned?"

"Of course, it depends on what you mean by that extraordinary word. Still, I'm almost sure not."

"If he asked you, would you marry him?"

"He's married, isn't he?"

"Suppose he said he'd get a divorce?"

"Oh, now then" Miss Paynton protested quite quietly "there's been nothing like that, you know!"

"I see" her companion said, following which they talked clothes, then went their separate ways, seemingly well satisfied with one another.

After Mr Middleton had come home, the day's work done, his wife waited till he'd had his tea and read the papers, she delayed until he'd taken his bath, and even so she did not speak before their dinner was over. Just as he was about to make himself scarce in the study with what he had brought back in his briefcase, however, Diana stopped her husband.

"Darling" she said "I know the other night I almost promised I would never mention this whole business again, but something else has happened now."

"Yes?" he answered in a resigned tone of voice, sitting down once more.

"Paula Paynton's been to me, exactly as I told you she probably might."

"If I remember, Diana, it was you proposed to call on Annabel's mother."

"I may have said so, dear. But if I did, the other was what I really expected."

"And I suppose she didn't just drop in to discuss this awful weather we've been having."

"She may have mentioned the rain, now I come to think, Arthur."

"Then out with it, Di. I've more than enough work to get through this evening. And don't torture me" he pleaded. "You know I'm on tenterhooks over the whole of the wretched misunderstanding."

"Oh you needn't be so alarmed" she told her husband. "You can be sure I saw Paula off, quite politely too, of course."

"Then what in the name of God, Di . . . ?"

"Now, now" she interrupted. "All in my own good time."

"I won't listen to any more of this nonsense" Mr Middleton announced, almost with passion. "Nor have I the leisure, even if you think you have."

"Very well" Diana told him, giving nothing away in the tone of voice she used, "Paula only came to ask weren't you seeing rather much of her precious little girl."

"But just because there has been a stupid accident, am I then to see no more of the child?"

"Oh you told me you've been having her out to lunch, darling. I admit that."

"Really, I must say very heavy weather is being made over some spilt coffee." Mr Middleton appeared to sulk. His wife closed her eyes and sighed.

"There was no mention of the skirt" she said at last.

"Who's been talking?" Arthur began again.

"You don't suppose I was so foolish as to ask Paula" Mrs Middleton replied. "No, naturally enough, when one goes out, one's seen."

"Doing what, good heavens?"

"Oh, Arthur, don't tell me there's been something else?"

He put his face in his hands.

"I shall go out of my mind" he said in a frantic voice. Mrs Middleton watched her husband with a quiet, appraising look.

"Don't worry" she told him. "I know my Paula. I've dealt with her, at least for the time being."

"So what's the position now?" Arthur demanded, rather more calmly.

"I suppose it all depends, quite a lot, on how much you intend to go on seeing the girl" his wife replied.

"Now look here, Di" he said. "You know how hard I work. I don't visit the club at night. I don't fish, I don't shoot. My one relaxation is to take a friend to lunch. And I always secretly wanted a daughter. Oh I'm not blaming you! Everyone realises what you went through having Peter. But what's wrong with my taking Ann out to a public place occasionally? It's all above board, surely? There's nothing clandestine about that, is there?"

"Well, I imagine Paula might prefer you to be more secret, anyway she said so."

"No, Di, this is a wild paradox you're putting forward."

"Well think, dear, and now go back to your briefcase. Try and see if you can do with perhaps a little bit less of Ann." She got up. She kissed him on the forehead. "There" she said. "But you do understand I had to warn, don't you?"

Mr Middleton asked the Paynton girl out to lunch at the usual time and place. He waited until they were seated at their table before he started.

"Your mother's been to see Di" he said.

"Oh?"

"About my taking you out to lunch like this."

"But how terribly disloyal of Mummy" Annabel wailed. "All I can say is, I hope you never treat Peter like that."

"In what way?"

"Because she's never said a word to me on the subject."

"Could it have made any difference if she had, Ann?"

"Of course not. But she would only have been polite if she did, don't you see?"

"A bit" he seemed to admit, with a measure of diffidence. "And do you think her going to Di has altered the situation?"

"What situation?" the young lady enquired, open-eyed. "There isn't one, is there?"

"I mean about your coming out to lunch occasionally" Mr Middleton explained.

"What does your wife say?"

"That we ought to be more secret."

"Here's a fine thing" Miss Paynton protested. "I shan't come at all if you even start to talk like this."

"Honestly, she did."

"Then I don't want to hear. I shall have to forget all of it, and I'm afraid I shan't find that easy."

"I'm very sorry, Ann."

"So you should be, for sure."

"What else can I do but apologise?"

"Just never mention it again."

"All right. But Ann, who's been talking, then?"

"How could I know?"

"D'you tell your mother when you come out with me?"

"I do not" she said. "Certain things have to be observed in family life" she announced, as though lecturing. "And if a girl's to say to her parents where she is every moment of the day, then there's absolutely no end to things."

"How did your mother find out then?"

"Perhaps Diana told her."

"No" Mr Middleton objected, in steadfast tones. "Di and I don't fib to one another."

"Well, I haven't said a word to a soul, no one" the girl maintained. "I can't understand it."

"And Arthur, have you spoken about us?"

"I have, yes, once" he admitted, obviously reluctant. "To a man."

"Who?"

"Oh, a very old friend" he said, airily. "Charles Addinsell . . . "

"The one who's taking Diana out five times in eight days?"

"Yes" he admitted, in a low voice.

"But how could you?"

"It was before he'd asked Diana out so often, you see."

"And what about my reputation?" she demanded.

"Now Annabel" he said. "We haven't done a thing, have we?"

"I'd like to get hold of that Mr Addinsell and tear his odious, prying eyes out, that's all."

"Because there's no harm in us, is there?" he went on.

"I'd thank you to know what you mean, Arthur."

"Well Charles talks, then Diana says this and that to me, she goes on about your reputation just as you do, – good heavens, to listen to 'em, we might spend all of every weekend in bed together."

"I must confess I don't think Diana's one to speak" the girl commented, thin-lipped.

"How's that?"

"When she obviously does, with this Mr Addinsell."

"Now look here, Ann, you go too far!"

"All right, but have you asked her?"

"Of course not!"

"Don't you discuss things with your wife?"

"Not those" he answered, beginning to seem shamefaced.

"I don't know about marriage" she protested. "Not yet! Still I can't think what could be better to talk about?"

"You will" he replied, almost with a smile, and appeared to regain his composure.

"But it's so important, Arthur."

"What is?"

"Sex. D'you honestly mean to tell me you don't know who your wife goes to bed with?"

"Listen, Ann" the man said in a tired voice. "You've got the whole of this wrong. All I maintain is, that one must be wicked to become jealous. D'you agree?"

"No."

"Very well, but I say it is so. We're all entitled to our opinions. And if, as I say, I'm wrong to be jealous, then I'd better not know whether I've grounds for jealousy. Do you see my position now?"

"I just can't understand why a man, like you describe you are, ever marries."

"But, Ann, the ideas one marries with, soon merge into the ideas one remains married on."

"I wouldn't know" she said.

"Perhaps not, but possibly you can imagine that."

"Well, I'm not sure, Arthur. And still, if a day or two ago you'd told me this Mr Addinsell would have been the one to tell darling Diana, and we can't know how much he's simply invented yet, then, with all your experience, I'd've said you were crazy."

"So would I" he admitted.

"Then it must be frightful to be married!"

"At times, possibly. Although things can be almost as bad when you're single, you must admit."

"So what ought one to do, Arthur?"

"Go on seeing each other."

"No, about marriage I mean, stupid!"

"Nothing, darling. Drift."

They both laughed. She told some funny stories about Campbell, after which both went back to work.

That night Mr Middleton failed to go off to his own room after dinner, as he usually did, but stayed by his wife, fidgeting with a newspaper on her sofa.

"What's this?" she asked. "Darling, have you stopped being married to your briefcase?"

"I can't make you out at all these days, my dear" the man complained.

"How's that?" she peaceably enquired.

"Di, I want us to have a little talk" he said.

"Well, all right."

"You're sure you won't mind, darling?"

"Why should I?" she asked. "I never interfere with your work, you know, and, if you wish to discuss anything, then here I am, as always."

"Yes" the husband assured her, in almost a reverential tone of voice. "But sometimes I wonder if it mustn't be most infernally dull for you."

"Oh well, what's best for Peter's sake suits me" she said. "I mean, your working so hard is to educate the boy, then give him a start in life. I keep the house going, there's a home for him when he's back in the holidays. That's all!" There was something defensive in her tone.

"But the way I'm wondering tonight is, do you have enough in your life, Di? What I've on my mind, – well look, we're not getting any younger, are we? I've such an awful lot to plough through every evening, that's my job, yet how about you? Can't be very gay for you, when I am at last back from the office?"

"Oh well, my dear, I suppose by now I've got used to it."

There was a pause. And then, quite suddenly, he spoke in what seemed to be acute annoyance.

"Yes, certainly" he said. "And all the same there's no call, is there, to go out five times with Charles Addinsell in eight days?"

"But, Arthur, I haven't" she protested with spirit.

He ticked the occasions off on his fingers, aloud.

"I'm rather sorry I told you, now, about when I did meet him" she answered. "Yet that's what we arranged, that we should tell each other, and we've kept it up for eighteen whole years" she said. "Still I don't agree going out to tea can be meeting someone, not in the sense we've continually used."

"Now, Di, you're deliberately trying to aggravate me."

"I'm not, darling. You know what we've always agreed. That we should each of us go whenever the other was invited."

"But I haven't been asked out! Not once, when you were with Charles."

"Please not to trip me up when I express myself" she said in a calm, collected voice. "Of course I meant, we ages ago settled that if one was asked without the other, then whoever was invited, accepted and went."

"But five times in eight days?" He sounded almost tearful.

"I haven't Arthur" she reasoned. "We never did count teas."

"What have I done?" he demanded.

"Only you know, my dear" she said.

"And what may that mean?"

"Just all it says" she answered.

"But darling, this is wrong, somehow. You're different suddenly. It's fantastic! What have you got against me all of a sudden?"

"Well, my dear" she explained, as though to a child "I didn't particularly want to say this, or perhaps not so soon, but Peter's growing up now, and we don't wish him to come back home to find what I did the other night, do we?"

"Diana, leaving everything else out for the moment, Peter's away at school when he is there, isn't he?"

"He won't always be" she replied. "When he's finished with his studies he'll live with us in the flat, until he finds a nice girl, settles down, and marries."

"Still, in fairness to me, whatever I may be supposed to have done, this is the holidays, now. He's away in Scotland or isn't he?"

"I know very well Peter's up fishing, Arthur. My very loneliness tells me that. All I'm trying is to keep a home together, for him to come back to."

"Well you won't do that if you're never in, yourself."

"Giving you your little opportunities, you mean?" she asked.

"Diana, you'll have me lose my temper in a minute."

"I'm sorry, darling, truly I am! But I didn't start this, did I?"

"Oh, everything is always my fault?"

"Now why do you say that?" she indignantly demanded. "So what have I done?"

"Only practically left home" he replied.

"I like that!" she complained. "Aren't I sitting in front of the fire here, now then?"

"You know how I mean."

"But I don't!" she protested. "You say I'm different, yet it's you who always are. And I can't imagine what I've done to deserve it!" There was a trace of tears in her tone.

"Oh forget everything" he said in a careless sort of voice. "I suppose I'm just upset."

"Now look, Arthur" she suggested. "If you feel like you say you do, why not have a word with Charles?"

"To tell the man he's seeing too much of my wife?"

"And what's wrong with that?" she demanded. "You're the husband, aren't you?"

"But he'd laugh me out of the club!"

"I don't understand, dear. Not one little bit! You say you're upset over my going to see Charles occasionally, and yet you don't care to discuss it with him?"

"I've already told you, Diana, haven't I? What more should I try and do?"

"But there's our old arrangement" she most reasonably argued. "We've always said, in fact you've just admitted, that whichever of us was asked could go without the other. So he invites me, and I accept!"

"Meaning you won't refuse unless I stop taking Ann out to an occasional lunch?"

"Well, what's wrong with that, Arthur?"

"It's inconceivable, that's all! Just goes to show the whole old mutual trust and confidence in our marriage has gone, the very thing I always thought and said was rather fine in us!"

"I'm not so sure about trust and confidence" she objected. "You don't seem at ease about what you appear to think Charles and I are doing."

"Well, now then, how are you behaving?"

"I don't know what you're attempting to impute, Arthur, but I don't like any of this, I may tell you!"

"Any more than you cared for what you dreamed up about Ann and me?"

"Which is entirely different" she quickly put in, with warmth. "You forget, my dear, I saw you! And with my own eyes."

"I don't know how else you could have seen?"

"Now, Arthur, enough, you're beginning to upset me! Oh why do you have to be so? Just when Peter had the ghastly accident and I come back and find you like I did!"

"Then you do admit all you're doing with Charles is so much retaliation?"

"I admit nothing of the kind" she replied with spirit. "He happens to be a very old, dear friend."

"And yet I introduced you originally?"

"Oh Arthur, you can be so aggravating. What difference does that make?"

"I should have thought a lot."

"Then go round and see him."

"We've been into that already" he wearily protested. "I can't. You'd have me a laughing stock!"

"I don't suppose any more than you've already made yourself with this Ann Paynton."

"What d'you maintain we ought to do, then? Separate?"

"Arthur!!" she screamed. "Arthur! You're never to say that again, d'you hear, even as a silly joke!"

"Very well" he said in a level voice. "I apologise."

"Oh damn" she remarked. "I think I'm going to cry!" Which she proceeded to do.

"Now darling" he said in the same voice. He came over. He began to rub a hand up and down her spine.

Through her tears she spluttered, "Why are you so horrid to me?"

"I'm sorry. There" he said, still rubbing.

She began to recover. "Forgive me. I never meant to" she announced and blew her nose.

He kissed the nape of her neck, tenderly.

She fumbled in the bag she had on her knee for a lipstick and came on Peter's latest letter.

"Oh I never showed you this, did I?" she asked in a voice already almost unmarked by tears. "It came by the second post. He's caught a fish."

"Not a salmon?" her husband fiercely demanded.

"Why, I'm not sure, what else? I mean that's what Dick has up there, isn't it?"

"A fifteen pounder" Mr Middleton quoted. "Why it's terrific! And only seventeen! This is wonderful news."

"Darling Peter" the mother said. "I always knew he would make a fisherman."

"His first salmon!" the father echoed.

"Darling" she next said to her husband. "You don't have to work tonight, do you? Let's go up now."

"Go up?" Mr Middleton laughed. "We're all on one floor here, you know."

She turned. She kissed him on the lips and took her time.

"Silly" she said, smiling. "Well, all right then! Next door."

After two nights and a day, Arthur Middleton got his friend Addinsell on the telephone and persuaded him to lunch at their club.

"I'm in trouble, Charles" he began, over a martini.

"Again?" Addinsell seemed rather guarded in his manner.

"Nothing's ever the same" his host groaned.

"Then have you been to bed with that girl, whatever her name is?"

"God, no. Who d'you take me for?"

"Why don't you? And get it over?"

"But I don't suppose she would, Charles. Look, old man, all this is beginning to get so serious it even affects my work."

"Things are bad, then! Always said you worked too hard, Arthur."

"What would you suggest? The bills have to be paid, don't they?"

"Relax."

"And how can I? See here, your wife died early, very tragic thing and all that, – oh I know it was hell for you at the time, – but, my God, after eighteen years of married life, you don't know how they can become!"

"I might be able to guess."

"Yes, Charles, but you can't tell until you're actually married to them for long," Mr Middleton said in a dry voice.

"Very possibly" the man agreed. "And so what's biting you at the moment?"

"Has Diana said anything?"

"Not a word."

"Well I asked you to take her out . . ."

"Which I have done" Mr Addinsell interrupted.

"Oh, I know, and thanks very much. But she hasn't said a word?"

"She wouldn't, Diana couldn't" his guest lied in a flat voice. "Her loyalty's like an oyster, and you'd cut yourself if you tried to open it with an opener."

"Yet there are men who deal with dozens a minute out of a barrel."

"Oh," Mr Addinsell objected "then, I imagine, they've all got their cards, are members of the Union. Any pearls they may find have to go to the credit of the Benefit Fund."

Arthur Middleton laughed, almost harshly. "Then Di's said nothing about Ann?"

"Never once referred to the girl."

"She has to me, Charles!"

"Only to be expected, after all."

"Yes, I suppose so" the husband admitted. "Yet, when you come to consider, just a coffee stain!"

"Difficult to see into a woman's mind, Arthur."

"It isn't for me, not where Ann is concerned with Di. Di tells me."

"Only natural after all."

"You think so? Even when there's nothing to it?"

"Isn't there?"

"Well, not so far. I mean, there's been nothing yet."

"Couldn't there be?"

"Not on her side. Honestly, Charles, you're becoming too much of an old cynic. The child's sweet!"

"Careful how you go, Arthur."

"What's your point now?"

"The sweeter they seem, the harder we fall."

"Well yes" Mr Middleton admitted, weakly.

"Now look around this room" Charles Addinsell appealed. The tall windows, leaning against rain, seemed to filter light back to dark bookcases from floor to ceiling to make a number of men, older than themselves, seated in deep, black armchairs with two waiters in attendance, appear as wraiths, thin before illness, and bloodless as cardboard. "Look at them. D'you suppose there isn't one not ready to think, or talk, of sex."

"By God, you alarm me!" Mr Middleton said lightly. "Well, all right" he went on "I admit I dream of going to bed with her all the time, morning, noon and night. So what?"

"Go on and do it. Get her off the system."

"But this might not be right for the child?"

"Let the girl decide that."

"And have Prior round one morning with his horsewhip?"

Mr Addinsell laughed. "She won't tell" he reassured. "They never do, they're always too ashamed."

"But I don't want her ashamed, Charles. That's just it, you see."

"You may not, but whether you like or not, one day she will be. And surely it's better for her that that shouldn't happen in wedlock?"

"Wedlock? Where did you get the frightful phrase?"

"In marriage then, which I always thought you took seriously."

"My God, I do" Mr Middleton admitted. "So much so, I've begun to think I ought to see less of Ann."

"How much d'you meet now?"

"Less, probably, than you imagine" the husband said with a dry voice.

"Which means?"

"Oh, about once a week."

"Only that!" Mr Addinsell cried, with the first sign he had shown of animation.

"Yes, I'd imagine it could sound seldom to you" Mr Middleton said, with some unction.

"Well, you can't see the girl much less, then."

"I'm beginning to feel I should cut down."

"But there's competition, must be."

"Don't!" Mr Middleton implored. He seemed genuinely upset. "I can't bear to think, please! I thought perhaps I might begin to forget her slowly, damn the child."

"I'm afraid you've got it rather badly."

"That's what my wife seems to suggest, as a matter of fact" Arthur admitted.

"And how d'you propose to go about this?"

"Precisely why I asked you out, Charles. You could do a damn good job of work for me here."

"Look, Arthur, you know from experience you can always count on me" the man said, without a smile.

"I thought I could ask her to a restaurant for a drink, and plead a very important lunch appointment. Then I'd look round and I'd see you having your drink near by. I would introduce you. And you could take her in for a meal. As a very old friend of Diana's you might tell her Di's been blowing off. Of course I would arrange with the headwaiter to settle it, if you signed the bill."

"Now Arthur. None of that! Although I can't ever forget what you did for me over that business with Penelope."

"No, I insist, Charles."

"We'll see" his guest said. "But Di's told me nothing, as I informed you."

"She has to me."

"And what am I to say to this Paynton girl?"

"You see, Charles, I can't speak to her, because nothing's happened yet! It would be presumption on my part. We just talk about the wind and the weather, now. I can't go to her and say my wife objects. She'd think I was insane."

"And I expect she'll slap my face!"

"She won't. But don't make her cry! Promise."

"Still don't know what I'm to say to her, old man."

"Tell Ann I have to meet her less, until this blows over. Make out you're an old friend of Di's, in whom she's confided. Why, old boy, to someone like you, it will be simple as falling off a log. It's just I can't discuss things with Ann because nothing's happened. After all, remember what you had me say to Penelope!"

Mr Addinsell left it that he could, and again, that he might not.

On their usual day, and the accustomed time and place, Arthur Middleton and Miss Paynton forgathered at the bar. It was cold and wet outside, but he seemed hot, almost bothered.

"I say, Ann" he said. "A frightful thing has cropped up. There's been a call from the Ministry and I've got to go today to lunch with the Permanent Secretary."

"Then where am I supposed to eat?" she cried.

"You know how things are" he apologised. He looked sharply round the room, could see no sign of Charles Addinsell. "Who can tell, we may run into someone" he added.

"Palm me off?" she wailed.

"Now you must forgive this. Of course I mean nothing of the kind, Ann. It's simply that I can't ignore this summons I've had, although I'm aware beforehand it will be a complete waste of time. Look, I could see the headwaiter and have him send your bill along."

"Oh Arthur" the girl broke out "I feel so awful, I really do! I can't imagine why I started to grumble. Somehow I felt as if I would never see you more!"

"Now, Ann, what is this? Aren't you well?"

"I'm quite all right, thank you" she said, rather severely. "Then when d'you have to go? At once?"

"How is the time?" he asked, glaring at the electric clock. After which he searched through that bar once more, from his stool. "Good Lord" he announced, so it seemed in great surprise "see who's here, old Charles! D'you know Charles Addinsell?" he asked the girl.

"The same one?"

"Yes."

"Of course I don't. Except what you've told me, Arthur."

"Then let's give him a drink."

After cordial introductions, plus some fervent small talk, Mr Middleton excused himself, without further explanation, and made off.

"Have another?" Charles Addinsell suggested.

"Oh, but I ought to go."

"Well then, one for the road."

"You are so kind. Might I really?"

"Good. Waiter, two more medium sherries. Waiter! Waiter! Good God, am I to have to shout? That's better. Yes, two medium sherries." He turned back to the girl. "Terrible job to get attention these days."

"Are you telling me" she agreed.

"Though, looking at you, I can see you don't suffer" he said.

"Oh, can't I!" she bridled, seemingly delighted. "Yet suppose I went up with you to a glove counter staffed by the usual girls, I'd let you do the asking."

He laughed. "You might be right at that" he said.

She frowned, stayed silent.

"Often come here?" he tried again.

"I always lunch out" she said, very grandly.

"Well, good luck" he proposed, raising the full glass.

"Thank you" she answered over hers.

"Known old Arthur long?"

"Ages!" she said "I was practically brought up with the son Peter, who's much younger than me, of course."

"At St Olaf's, isn't it, where I was with Arthur?"

"Then you have known him a long time!"

"Doesn't seem like that."

"Really?" she asked in a cool, grand tone.

"So you've known Diana, too, for quite a bit?"

"Darling Di" Miss Paynton assented.

"Wonderful woman" Charles mused aloud, in a reflective sort of voice.

"Then you've been friends with her for a whole long while, as well?"

"The usual thing" the man told Ann. "Arthur was just about my best friend, and I was in love with Di before he married her."

"But how extraordinary!" Miss Paynton exclaimed, in a warmer manner than she had yet assumed.

"So so" Addinsell grunted.

She smiled with obvious malice at his eyes.

"You still don't sound very pleased!"

He studied the girl coldly.

"I suppose that's a thing could happen to any one of us" he replied.

"I'm sorry" she said, almost humane. "I didn't mean to seem as if . . ."

"Don't worry" he interrupted, giving Ann his first smile. This always seemed to make an impression of extraordinary charm and frankness, because it broke up his somewhat severe, handsome middle-aged features.

"One never sees anyone one knows, any more, in these places" he tried once again.

"Well, to be absolutely truthful" she admitted in a gayer voice "I've not met many. I simply haven't had time yet."

"Yes, pretty few dances these days."

"It's quite a problem for a girl, oh yes."

"Yet I suppose Prior and Paula still have young people in?"

"Of course you know Mummy and Dads! But who can afford much of that nowadays?"

"Your parents can't be as expensive as you make out, surely?"

She gaily giggled.

"You are awful!" Miss Paynton protested. "Don't dare to pretend my remark meant anything of the sort!"

He smiled. "Sorry, and all" he said.

"And so you should be" she commented, indulgently forgiving.

"Have one more?"

"What about you?" she temporised.

"I'm going to."

"Well, perhaps. Then I'll simply have to fly."

They were silent while he ordered, and obtained, the drinks.

"But you can't tell me that a man like you, with all your friends, ever has a casual, empty moment?" she proposed, in what appeared to be genuine friendliness.

"Oh, don't I" he objected. "What with the last show and all, many of 'em are dead by now."

"Yes, with two wars and everything in between, your generation's had quite a pasting."

"Not quite so old as that, just yet" he told her, with a smile. "Arthur and I were still at school in the first do."

"Oh, what can you think?" she cried. "How ridiculous!" She blushed.

"Not at all. Most natural; forget it. Look, what about a spot of lunch. Do one very well at this place."

"Oh, I often come here" she boasted. "But after what I said? I mean I don't deserve . . ." she went on in a more natural way than previously. "And I did ought to be getting along. As a matter of fact we've rather a marvellous arrangement at our office about the lunch hour." Talking hard now, she proceeded to tell Addinsell a good deal on the subject of her work. In the end they walked through to the restaurant without another mention of their lunch.

"What would you like to have?" he enquired.

"Oh no, I couldn't."

"Not even lion's drink?"

"No, no, I'd be drunk!"

"It's water."

"Oh you are silly" she giggled. "I never heard that one before. Yes, I think I'd better."

"All right far as I'm concerned."

"No, water really, please!"

"Suit yourself" he agreed, then proceeded to order an expensive meal.

"Saw old Diana the other day" he began once more, but this time without looking at the girl.

"You did?"

"Yes" he agreed, eyes averted.

"Well what's strange about that?" she demanded, in rather a nervous voice.

"Seemed a bit upset" Mr Addinsell pronounced, gravely regarding the young lady for once.

"But how extraordinary" Miss Paynton exclaimed. "She's never said anything to me."

"Hasn't she?"

"What d'you mean?" Ann almost quavered, then seemed to recover. "Oh well she wouldn't, you understand. Not to a woman who is, after all, of another generation. Look" she broke out. "Over there. No, there! Isn't that the film star, Jack Cole?"

"I wouldn't know. Don't go to 'em."

"Oh Mr Addinsell, what you miss" she almost cooed, and yet seemed alerted, defensive.

"Now, why don't you just call me Charles?"

"May I?"

"And can I reciprocate with Ann?"

"Of course." She spoke with complete unconcern. "Everyone uses Christian names nowadays, at least in my generation. It just doesn't mean a thing" she threw in. "D'you know, I think he is Jack Cole!"

"Who's he appeared with?"

"Oh Jack Cole's simply too terrific for words. He's slaying!"

"How d'you find Arthur's been these last few days, Ann?"

"Why just splendid, Mr Addinsell."

"Charles."

"Charles!"

"Thought he could have been a bit upset, I think myself."

"Oh, poor Arthur! And, now, is that Cicely Amor, can it be, he's talking to?"

"The blonde?" Charles demanded, with animation. He looked round at once. He saw this actor, whom he knew by sight, was talking to the cigarette girl, a negress.

Miss Paynton began to giggle, eyes brimming.

"By Jove" he said, and laughed.

The young lady giggled still more.

"Aren't I a silly juggins?" he exclaimed, apparently delighted. "Well, we won't talk about them any more, shall we?"

"What d'you mean?" she asked, serious again at once.

"That, dammit, that this fish is really rather good, though as host I say as shouldn't."

After which they got along very well, talking on indifferent subjects.

When she thanked him and was about to leave, Mr Addinsell said, "Meet again?"

"We'll see" she replied smiling.

"Ring you up?"

"How will you know my number?"

"I could ask Arthur."

"No, don't do that" and she then and there gave it to him. "Now I must fly. So thanks so much! Goodbye" she told him in expiring tones, and made off fast.

Her day's work done, Annabel Paynton had a drink in the pub outside the office with her closest confidante, Miss Claire Belaine.

"Well darling!" she said. "Only imagine, but I rather fancy it's happened all over again!"

"My dear, you're impossible" the girl replied, with calm.

"Aren't I? But you don't really think I am, do you?"

"Well, first tell me more."

"As a matter of fact, he's a friend of the other."

"Of the middle-aged one?"

"That's right."

"Then are you being handed on, Ann?"

"Nothing like it!" Miss Paynton laughed, with confidence. "No, Arthur – there I go once more – was called away to a sudden conference at the Ministry, you know how terribly high up he is, and this friend happened to look in at the bar of our restaurant and I was introduced, to this second one I mean, the one I'm telling you about."

"Married?"

"I've made a few enquiries. No, as a matter of plain fact he's a widower with a child, a boy of eight."

"And dark and handsome?"

"Oh Claire" Ann breathed "you've no conception!"

"Have I met him?"

"I'm almost certain you never have, but of course I can't give you his name, not just yet!"

"If he's unmarried there's no harm, surely?"

"Why, I suppose so. Claire, I hadn't thought! How odd" she

mused aloud. "But I keep this passion for secrecy. Mummy, I expect." Then she whispered the name.

"I've never even heard of him" Claire announced.

"Is there any reason why you should, darling?"

"I don't know, Ann. I didn't mean to sound important. Then how d'you feel about this Arthur, now?"

"I can't be sure" Miss Paynton replied with caution. "You see he hardly ever seems to talk about himself, which rather makes me weary, if you know what I mean." She laughed selfconsciously.

"Oh I like someone who can manage to listen."

"And so do I, of course. But he doesn't so to speak tell one."

"Unlike Campbell?"

"Most" Ann laughed.

"Perhaps it's his age?"

"But he isn't really old, Claire."

"Possibly not. Still he may find that holds him in."

Miss Paynton glanced in a wary way at her companion.

"No, as he's talking, he compares everything with about twenty years ago" she said, rather fast.

"Well, it may be he gave up being alive that long ago."

"When he married? Shall I find it in all my middle-aged men? How grim!"

"I think they batten on one."

"Why, you dark horse, how d'you know?"

"Don't your parents batten on you?"

"I seem to see what you mean, Claire dear. Oh, it's not much of a prospect, then, or is it?"

"Which has been my point all along!"

"But one's got to do something" Miss Paynton protested and laughed. And they went on to discuss underclothes, with spirit.

That night, after Mr Middleton, having dined, had retired to his own room with the briefcase, Diana several times approached the telephone without, however, actually taking the receiver off its cradle.

She also moved around her room, picked up illustrated papers only to put them down again, opened two novels but to throw these away, and at last did something she seldom used to do, bearded her husband in his den before she went to bed.

"I'm so bored, darling" she said, entering without apology. "So flat, down!"

"Hullo" he greeted Diana quite warmly. "Now what does this mean? Servant troubles getting less?"

"Don't be absurd, my dear" she answered. "Why does a wife, who copes, have to listen to such silliness? No, I've nothing to do. I'm bored stiff."

"Haven't you a book?"

"Arthur, I'm quite constipated with all the novels I read."

"Then why don't you go out?"

"Who with?"

"Charles Addinsell not rung up of late?" he asked, keeping voice and face straight.

"Don't be ridiculous, darling" she said, and sat down rather heavily opposite.

"I see" he answered, with a small show of irritation.

"Well, if you do, I don't" she objected, in a flat tone. "Arthur, listen to me! Can we go on like this?"

"Why, what is it now?" he cried irritably. "What on earth d'you mean?"

"Oh I know I'm being vile" Diana wailed. "But can all your terrific work be worth the candle?"

"You don't suppose I like slavery for its own sake, surely to goodness!"

"Sometimes I simply wonder, Arthur."

"Is that all the thanks one gets?"

"We've our own lives to live after all, still, haven't we?"

"And what about Peter? He has to be paid for, and educated; you know it as well as I do!"

"Occasionally I ask myself if the darling wouldn't be better off in a council school."

"Diana! Stop! He'd never in after life forgive us if I didn't give him the start I got from my father."

"And where did that land you?"

"No really, Diana" her husband protested, but with some signs, at last, of unease "what are you trying to insinuate? That we've been failures?"

"Not at all" she protested. "Just, we might have gone somewhere further, that's all!"

"Where then?"

"Don't ask me. It's for the man to choose his own job."

"And how much choice is there, nowadays?"

"I couldn't say, of course, Arthur" she admitted with a certain show of reason. "Yet, d'you really think we are making the best of our lives?"

"Darling" he said "I'm doing all I can!"

"I know" she agreed. "But couldn't you do something else?"

"Such as?" he demanded, in a weak voice.

"How can I tell?" she protested once more.

He came over to sit on the arm of her chair.

"Darling, what is this?" he asked gently.

"Oh just nothing. I'm so bored" she repeated, almost in a whisper.

"Di, you don't really mean all you've just said?"

"Yes, darling, I do, but it doesn't matter, you're to pay no attention."

"On the contrary" he protested "if that is so, then everything matters very much. What concerns me is your happiness, your welfare, my dear."

"Does it?"

"How d'you feel in yourself?" he elaborated. "Every day!" he added.

Picking up his hand from off her shoulder, she kissed the wrist.

"Darling darling" she said.

"Of course that's so" he consented. "Have I ever given you cause to fear, or even doubt? You mustn't be down like this. Why not go out? You know I'm stuck here."

"Who with?"

"Well, after all, as I said before, there's old Charles."

"He hasn't rung up in a week, Arthur!"

"Then just you ring him!"

"Oh but Arthur, that's to make oneself cheap!"

"You cheap? My dear, you couldn't, not with that man" he protested.

"Now you shan't grow nasty once more about dear Charles" she sadly told her husband. "No" she added "I must not get on to him. I still have my pride."

"Then what do you propose, dear?"

"Arthur, couldn't we have an early night tonight? Won't you come along to bed, now? I get so hipped lying there, waiting for you!" She smiled up into his eyes. "Come on, then" she said, and squeezed his hand.

He kissed her with what seemed to be restraint.

"Very well, for this once" he agreed, upon which they went off arm in arm, immediately.

Some five days later the two girls met, by appointment, in their usual pub.

"Then how are you going along, Ann?" Miss Belaine enquired.

"How is who getting on?" she countered.

"I'm sorry" the confidante apologised. "What I meant was, have you heard any more of Arthur?"

"He's not quite the point he was, is he, darling?" Miss Paynton replied. "I believe I told you he has a friend who's newly appeared on the scene."

"Well anyway, what's your news?"

Ann giggled. "I've been dropped" she said. "Like a hot brick."

"By both of them?"

"Oh, the other had me to tea at a hotel since I saw you last, and he, at least, does show signs of being able to talk about himself, but of Arthur, not a word!"

"He may have the wind up."

"Of his wife?"

"No, about himself."

"I only wish he could" Annabel Paynton tiredly complained. "He's nothing but a bore the way he is now, or was, because, of course I haven't seen him."

"So he's out, where you're concerned?"

"Out? I never said that! All I say is, we should have as many people round us as we can, to pretend to choose from. You always maintain one must keep oneself to oneself and I expect you skip a lot of pain and worry that way. My theory is, I'm expendable, up to a certain point, of course."

"So you've said before, Ann. But I argue that if you pursue this, you'll make the men you go out with expendable, too."

"The moment they invite me, they let themselves in for that, don't they?"

"And what do they expect in return?" Miss Belaine enquired, with a small frown.

"Why bed, of course."

"Do they get it?"

Miss Paynton giggled. "Strictly confidentially, no" she said. "At least, not yet, with me. You know that."

"Which is where we disagree" Claire announced, but in rather a doubtful voice. "With precautions, of course, I don't see what difference it can make."

"And you who always swore you never did!"

"I don't, Ann."

"So where are you, if you go out with a married man?"

"I haven't."

"Then d'you think one ought to pay them for the dinner by going to bed with them, supposing you accepted?"

"Not necessarily, Ann. You're too literal. It might only make them miserable."

"Well, darling, I don't believe things quite work out like you've just described."

"I dare say not" Miss Belaine assented. "Yet, whichever way one goes about things, one makes the creatures expendable."

"Which I say we are, too. In any case, they ask for what they get by inviting us out, as I've just told you."

"For bed?"

"Oh, I expect. No, what I meant is, they make themselves expendable the minute they ask one out."

"And supposing one falls in love with them?"

"But, Claire, we mustn't run away from life, not at our age! If we've got to fall in love, we just do."

"D'you think this Arthur's in love with you?"

"Doesn't look like it, does he, and frankly, at the moment, I couldn't care less."

"Oh well, let me know what happens in three weeks' time, Ann."

"Three days, you mean! You don't propose to suddenly stop listening, do you?"

They laughed, finished their drinks, and went separate ways.

Miss Paynton had agreed to meet Charles Addinsell for lunch and somehow they, almost at once, got into a discussion. He'd been speaking against wives.

"The whole thing's no good" he wound up, after being very vague.

"But, Charles, I can't follow at all" she protested. "This might become very important for me, some time. Why not?"

"You wait."

"What on earth for, Charles?"

"Almost impossible to describe."

"Excuse me if this is personal" she put forward "but did your wife leave you, or something?"

"No."

"Then how?"

"She died."

"Oh, good heavens, I do apologise. What was her name?"

"Penelope."

"Now that's an absolutely heavenly name! So well?"

"She just died, Ann."

"Surely to goodness you can't have it against her, Charles?"

"You've never been left with a child on your hands, have you?"

"Well, no, I suppose not."

"So there you are."

"But you mustn't hold it against your wonderful Penelope."

"Don't know what you mean. No one's fault when they die in bed, is it? Can't see how that could be?"

"Then why not marry a second time?" Ann asked, in a bewildered voice. "Another mother for your child?"

"Might die again" the man replied, with obvious distaste.

"Oh, no!" she cried.

"Not much use for poor little Joe if she did, after all?"

"I suppose not, Charles. Yet there's no reason she should, is there?"

"Oh none" he appeared to agree. "Still, that's all a part of what life has in store for one."

"Now Charles!" she protested.

"You're young still" he said, in a menacing sort of fashion.

"But it's so hideous!"

"Yes" he assented.

"About your wife, I mean. How did she die, if I may ask?"

"In childbirth."

"Yet that's the finest sort of death for a woman, surely, or so they used to say, didn't they?"

"Don't know."

"And you just blame her for it? Oh, Charles! Really, then, we can't ever seem to do right in life, can we?"

"Of course I never have blamed" he said, with obvious petulance. "Poor darling, she couldn't help going like that" he explained. "Not her fault, good God! If anything, might have been mine, or equally the fault of each of us, in actual practice. No, what I have against living, is the dirty tricks fate has in store. No good blinking facts. Do better to realise, they probably will be coming to you. I couldn't stand a second kick in the pants of the kind."

"But if you've already had one really terrible misfortune, aren't the chances against another, Charles?"

"Same as with roulette" he answered. "When you're at the tables, identical numbers will keep cropping up!"

"Oh, surely that's most terribly gloomy."

"Depends on how you play" Mr Addinsell replied. "If you're on a number and there's a run on zero, where are you then?"

"I've never even seen the game."

"Well you can back any number up to thirty seven, and in combinations, but if the ball falls into a slot on the wheel which is marked nought, everyone loses who hasn't betted on zero."

"I still can't seem to see why a person should want to put their money on nothing."

"Because it's precisely what they may get, Ann!"

"Oh, I didn't mean at your silly gambling game. In life, I was talking about."

"I'm no Omar Khayyam" Mr Addinsell gravely told this girl. "But the spin of the wheel is all any one of us can expect."

"So you say that I, for instance, oughtn't to marry on account of what so tragically happened to you and yours?"

"Of course not!" he protested with warmth. "Never in the world! Was speaking selfishly."

"Terribly sad for you, then" she murmured, eyes downcast.

"One gets used to it" he said. "To anything." Then he added with a sly smile "Can even have compensations, sometimes."

"That you do realise, once and for all, things for you can't ever become worse?" she asked, looking at him again.

"It could be better than that" he drily answered.

"How then, Charles?"

"Persistent, aren't you!"

"I'm sorry! I realise I become an awful bore, soon as ever I grow interested. I didn't intend to be a nuisance!"

"Hey, what are you saying?" Charles demanded. "Come off it! If I spoke out of turn, let me apologise."

"You didn't."

"Pretty sure I did. Look, I take it all back! I've a mistaken sense of humour."

"Then you're just laughing at me?"

"Don't follow what you mean, Ann."

"I can't see your jokes, that's all" she announced, in a most dignified way.

"My dear, I do apologise, I do really" he said, in the nearest approach to the abject he could probably manage.

"For what?" she enquired, and seemed mollified.

"For anything and everything" he handsomely replied. There was a pause.

"So you don't feel you can be happy ever again, is that it?" she asked.

"Hardly."

"But it's outrageous!" she protested. "Look at you! With so many years to see forward to, to live a full life in!"

"Maybe you misunderstood" he said, in a flat voice. "I told you before there could be consolations, Ann."

"D'you mean to sit and tell me to my face you're referring to just squalid affairs?" she cried with a great show of indignation. "You, a man with a boy of eight!"

"Not guilty" he replied, and seemed quietly amused. "All I tried to say was, one could still have friends."

"Oh friends!" she broke out. "I have tons of those, and yet what earthly use are they to me."

"The salt of life" he suggested with a sly smile.

"Are you honestly trying, after all your experiences, to propose that I've nothing more than friendships in the years I still have to live?"

"My point was and is, stay chary of your commitments, Ann."

"Well, of course. Who isn't?"

"And don't believe it's to be a bed of roses."

"How could I? What sort of a person d'you suppose I am? Charles, I'm surely still all right in my head!"

"You're always getting away beyond me" he mildly complained. "All I meant was, I suppose, just don't expect too much."

"And mustn't I even hope for the best?" she wailed.

"Can't stop people hoping" he agreed. "Don't advise you to, all the same."

"You are wonderfully cheering, aren't you, Charles?"

"Only speak to the truth as I know it" he answered with a sort of dignity.

There was another pause.

"I'm sure I don't know where I'm going to be, now, with my life" Miss Paynton at last complained, in a child's voice.

"Never let anything get you down" the man advised.

"In which case, you can't remember much of what you felt at my age."

"Not sure I do, at that."

"Weren't you ever miserable then, Charles?"

"I expect so. Tolerably."

"And so what has anyone to live for?"

"Blessed if I know."

"But supposing you were a girl?" Miss Paynton demanded, with insistence.

"I'm not."

"Well, I imagine I realised that" she countered. "Yet, if you were, would you really warn a woman against looking forward to her own children."

"They can always die, too."

"In a bomb explosion, you mean?"

"Not necessarily" he said.

"Oh but fifty years ago they died like flies, quite naturally!" Ann exploded. "Doctors have changed all that! I don't suppose any number of bombs nowadays could kill the millions of people that used to go just from disease."

"People still die, all the same" Mr Addinsell objected.

"Then am I not to love anyone because, like all of us, they've got to die some time?"

"Don't know."

"But, please, you do truly love your Joe, don't you?"

"Certainly."

"And he's still alive and kicking, isn't he?"

"Well, yes."

"Then are you going to love him less for that?"

"I am. You see, Ann, on account of if he died."

"But, Charles, are you saying I oughtn't to have children because they might die."

"My point is, love no one too much, in case they do."

"No, no" she protested. "I'd be bound to love my own children."

"Anyway" he said, with a sort of finality "there's very little anyone can do about things."

His face, which she was watching, took on a look of great sadness. She then changed the conversation adroitly and they talked of musical comedy until the time came for her to go back, late, to work.

Diana Middleton persuaded her husband to take her out to dinner, a thing he was usually unwilling to do.

"I'm sorry to be disagreeable again, darling" she said, as soon as they'd had a few drinks at the restaurant to which he'd taken Ann "but I've gone to see Paula myself, this time."

"You have?"

"Yes, darling."

"Well, what on earth for?"

"It's simply this" she told Arthur. "I felt I had to warn Paula that Charles was seeing too much of her Ann."

"And you got me out to tell that?" he asked, in level tones.

"I did, darling."

"Well, what did you say to the woman?"

"But I've just explained!"

"I mean, how did you put it?" Mr Middleton demanded, as if wearily, of his wife.

"I thought you might be rather angry with me" she admitted.

"What have I said now?" he enquired.

"You're being a bit difficult, you know, darling" Diana announced.

The husband rubbed the palm of his hand all over his face, starting with the forehead.

"In what way?" he asked.

"Oh, am I being very tiresome?" she wanted to be told. "No, but I feel I do have a certain responsibility to the child."

"Why?" he asked.

"Well, Paula's my oldest friend, although we aren't quite that, perhaps any more, now, and you did, forgive me, seduce Ann, after all!" Diana sounded rather breathless.

"You mean you've quarrelled with Paula?"

"So you don't deny it?"

"With my last dying word!" Mr Middleton informed his wife, in a voice which could have been called expiring.

"I'm sorry, my dear" his spouse brought out, with what, she obviously thought, was sweet reasonableness. "But I had to, didn't I? One has certain duties, after all."

"I can't make a word of this out, Diana."

"But you must understand how I did. I don't want you upset, all the same."

"It would be so much easier if you consented not to talk in riddles, dear."

"Oh" Mrs Middleton commented in a gay, bright voice "I don't wish, or choose, to go into the whole old business anew. Above all, I wouldn't want you provoked, darling. Yet you should admit it was the only thing I could do."

"What, I'm getting almost hoarse with asking?"

"Why, tell her, of course."

"In which way?"

"How can that matter?" Mrs Middleton demanded innocently of her husband. "I'm trying my best to keep calm, dearest. Oh, was it so very awful in me to drag you out like this?"

"After nineteen years of married life" he commented "I've learnt to let you take your time."

"Eighteen years" she corrected him.

"Yes, dear" he replied with patience, and what seemed to be humility.

"Well of course all I said was, it had come to my knowledge that Ann was going out so much with Charles, and that much as I dote on the man, I could only think the whole thing quite unsuitable, and although I'd resented her coming to me earlier about her girl and you, which I know to be true but how was I to admit that to Paula, what wife would, – where am I? – oh well, all I said was, and you must admit I couldn't not, was simply that Ann would set all the old tongues wagging."

"And has she?"

"Not perhaps yet. But she will."

"And how often does she really go out with Charles?" Mr Middleton enquired, in obvious disquiet.

"The whole time."

"Then she's a little bitch" the husband pronounced. "That's all I can say, a little bitch" he repeated, firmly.

"Oh, I'm so sorry about all of this" the wife wailed.

"Why?"

"Well, of course, I wasn't exactly heartbroken to be able to go to Paula after she'd been to me originally in that peculiarly reprehensible way, but how else can one prevent things turning out in quite such a revolting fashion?"

"And I who imagined Charles Addinsell my dearest friend!" Mr Middleton remarked in a grieving voice, it seemed almost at random.

"D'you blame him, then?" his wife asked.

"Who'd have ever believed it?"

"So, Arthur, you openly confess you're jealous, is that it?"

"Hey, what's this?" he demanded as though he'd had a rude awakening.

"I don't know yet" she announced, with menace in her voice.

"All I mean is" her husband patiently explained "it must be an entirely different matter, my taking the girl out and a man like Charles to do so. I'm married, for one thing. Everyone knows I'm safe as houses. Whereas Charles, well, he's just a voluptuary."

"What's that, darling?"

"Oh well, let it pass. I'm sorry I ever introduced them, now."

"You did! But how tiresomely stupid of you, Arthur. You should have known you'd lose her by so doing!"

"You can't lose what you haven't got" the husband objected.

"We won't go into that again. Not in this crowded place! Yet why are you still sorry?"

"I am for little Ann, because Charles is the man he's turned out to be."

"I see, Arthur. So you don't meet Ann, now?"

"No. And do you ever see Charles?"

"No more, no more!" his wife wailed comically. At which they both laughed in a rather shamefaced way at each other.

"In spite of all your tricks I love you, darling" Mr Middleton told his wife.

"You're a wicked old romantic" she said, beaming back at him.

"Enough of a one to put a spoke in your works every now and again."

"Oh don't worry" she announced. "I haven't done with Charles yet, not by a long chalk!"

"Steady on! You're playing with fire there."

"I wouldn't mind if it was hell's own flames, dearest. It seems someone thinks they're making a donkey out of me."

"But you can't imagine I introduced an innocent little thing like Ann to Charles just so you should see less of him?"

"Innocent? Ann! No, it's she is at the back of all this."

"How, darling?"

"How would you feel, if you were a woman, about the girl who was trying to take away your husband and your friend, all in the one go?"

"Much as I do feel about Charles" he answered reasonably. "With you" he added, to make doubly clear, perhaps.

"And Ann?" she demanded.

"I was referring to Charles" her husband countered.

"But, my dear, we always had our great arrangement" Diana said. "The one could go out when the other wasn't asked."

"So what, my dear?"

"Why, simply that you never kept to it, and I did, which is all!"

"Now, my love," he protested, with heat "you know this simply isn't true! When did I ever take Ann out to lunch any time you and I were both invited?"

"Have you once rung me up, before, to see if anyone had phoned?"

"But I used to ring Ann first thing, soon as ever I got to the office after seeing you over breakfast."

"Oh Arthur, first thing! What can your telephone girl have thought? Just warm from our bed!"

"She wasn't."

"No please, don't try to laugh this off, I'm serious! Didn't you even open your letters first?"

"When all's said and done, it was only once a week. And I always used to read them while I was talking with Ann."

"You can't have had such a lot to say to each other then?" Mrs Middleton asked, in a doubtful voice.

"Only to invite her out to lunch, Diana."

"And once, which is the only time I know about, to dinner, exactly when I was supposed to be on the train to Scotland with your own son."

"So you maintain you've never been to dinner with Charles?"

"That's an entirely different kettle of fish."

"I'll say it is" the husband protested, almost with violence.

"Now, darling" she begged him. "Don't let's go into all this yet again. You're entirely in the wrong, and it can be so painful."

"Oh very well, dear" he said, as if in resignation.

"Then what d'you propose to do about things?" she demanded.

"After all that's occurred I must say I obviously can't take Ann out, even once more. If anyone can be said to have learnt a hard lesson, then it's me" the man said.

"How, darling?"

"But my dear" he protested "your suspicions even over the ordinary accident Ann and I had, have simply made me ill!"

"And so they ought! Yet you don't intend to sit idly by under this, do you, Arthur?"

"Then what do you propose?"

"I don't know" she said.

"Isn't there something I could do, darling" he pleaded.

"I must think" she answered, then immediately went on. "You should ask Ann out again" Mrs Middleton propounded. "Not at night, of course. Never that! You must promise me faithfully, Arthur, you'll never again invite her on an evening?"

"Certainly" he said.

"You promise?"

"I swear."

"Very well then, you will have to give Ann lunch. And don't enjoy it, mind! Because I shall simply have to go up to Dick's for a few days to be with Peter, too unfair to leave the boy alone any longer. So let me tell you, dear. If, when I come back, I find any funny business, I shall just be distraught, darling, and you know from experience what that can mean! I might even try reprisals."

"Yes, dear."

"Then just remember! Yes, I feel you should take her out to lunch, once more. We owe as much, at least, to Paula."

"Yes, darling. And what do I say?" the husband asked.

"Not too much" Mrs Middleton replied. "Of course, for a start, you should warn Ann against Charles."

"And then?"

"Isn't that simply enough, Arthur? What else could you wish?"

"It wasn't me" he explained. "It happened to be you, I thought, wanted that I should do more."

"Do more? Please be careful what you're saying!"

"I simply imagined you had a plan, I'd an idea you knew what else you wished me to put over."

"Well of course I do" Mrs Middleton admitted. "Only I find it so difficult to say in words."

"Should I suggest I'd not be able to face old Prior, if he came after me with a horsewhip, for introducing his daughter to a man like Charles?"

"My dear" she protested "please don't be so ridiculous! How can you imagine she'd care two hoots even if poor Prior tarred and feathered you!"

"I see, darling" he humbly admitted.

"At one time I thought you could say Charles was ill, had T.B., or something. And then I saw, at once, that that would be no good, the

136

desperate little thing would go like mad for a sick man, she'd think her chances even better. No, tell her Charles is only interested in women very much older than himself, that he had this passion when he was a boy, as so many of them do, and, of course, in those days, his women weren't so very old yet. Then, Arthur, you must explain how he has never been able to grow out of this peculiar habit, that he's been to all sorts and kinds of psychoanalysts, and the only advice they've any of them been able to give the poor man, was that he should, so to speak, try himself out, every now and again, on a girl who is very considerably, even absurdly, younger than he is, now."

"Will Ann believe me?"

"Why not, if she has before, dear? In any case, who's she got to check up with? She can't go to Paula, at this late date."

"I suppose not."

"Besides, Arthur, think how ridiculous she would look going to any older woman to ask a question of that kind. It would give her whole squalid little game away."

"She told me she only liked older men."

"Oh she did, did she?" Mrs Middleton snorted. "Then, if she's said anything else of that sort, I'll thank you kindly not to tell your own wife, which I still am! One has to keep certain standards in married life, after all."

"Very well, darling."

"You will, then?" she asked.

"I shall" Mr Middleton replied, without any show of enthusiasm. After which his wife changed the subject. She spoke at length, and with fervour, of Peter, and, afterwards, of their friends, in both of which topics Arthur Middleton joined wholeheartedly.

When they came home, it was plain the two of them had had, on the whole, a very pleasant evening.

The next day, therefore, Mr Middleton directed the telephone girl, as soon as he was in his office, to ring Ann Paynton and ask if the young lady would speak with him.

When the instrument tinkled at his right hand, he raised its receiver rather slowly. He listened into a silence.

"Ann, this is me" he said at last, in an almost panic-stricken way.

"Oh hullo!" her voice came loud and unattached, then broke into a carefree, boisterous little laugh.

"You're different" he announced.

"Am I?" she replied.

"Sound cheerful enough!"

"Good" she said.

"What have you been doing with yourself, dear Ann?"

"Oh well, I've been up and about."

"Had yourself a nice time?"

"As a matter of fact, quite, thanks."

"Splendid" the man said, soberly. "Seen anyone I know?"

"You're a stranger these days" Miss Paynton countered at once.

"You don't mind my ringing up like this?" he then asked.

"Why no, how should I?"

"Perhaps I just thought you didn't sound too pleased."

"I'm always glad to hear from you, Arthur" she said quietly.

"D'you think we could possibly take lunch together again?"

"I might."

"You don't, quite, seem what is called impatient, Ann."

"It isn't that at all" she explained, with her far away voice. "I happen to be rather full, you see."

"Could you manage Tuesday?"

"This week, or next?"

"Tomorrow."

"Just let me look at my book. Yes, as a matter of fact, I find I can."

"Fine. And same time and place?"

"That will be heaven" she said, in a disinterested way. Then with a suggestion of laughter, she asked "Are you sure it will be all right?"

"Yes" Mr Middleton said.

When he put back the receiver he was frowning.

By the time they were seated at their usual table in the restaurant, Arthur Middleton was palpably nervous, while Ann behaved with what was, for her, an unusual calm.

"I never apologised for leaving like I did, the last time" he began.

"No, you haven't rung up, have you?" Miss Paynton replied.

"I've been rather rushed lately, Ann."

"I envy the way you can telephone in your office, merely by telling the girl to get any person you want. Where I am, one has to go through a perfect rigmarole, over private calls."

While she told him this, she was examining the other guests with a very languid eye.

"D'you do it much, then?" he enquired.

"Arthur" she asked, and still did not seem to bother to look at the man, "would you advise me to move, change over into something better?"

"Hard to say. Most people get fed up with their jobs every so often. Haven't you been out much lately?"

She gave him what appeared to be a reproachful glance.

"Well, I must say" she said "you don't seem very interested in my problems."

"Why, I'd just asked, Ann, if you'd led a gay life of late!"

"Which might be a peculiar way of putting things, or isn't it? Oh, if you mean have I been out" she explained, back again now at her scrutiny of the people in this great room "if that's what you're trying to say, well yes, I have. No, as for a gay life I was referring to my career."

"But for someone as beautiful as you, that must mean marriage."

Miss Paynton turned her eyes on him, began to show a trifle more animation.

"Which I always think is a bit patronising to say to a girl" she complained, with a long-suffering air. "Don't men get wed? Isn't that just as important for them, too?"

"I'll say it is! Ann, you misunderstood me."

"How did I?"

There was a pause in which he gazed at the girl with obvious anxiety, and she looked down at her plate.

"Oh you do look so wonderful, I'd forgotten!" he said at last.

"Had you?"

"No, no, not that" he corrected. "I don't think it's ever been out of my mind, not since the rabbit hutch. Ah, Ann, you're ravishing, this afternoon!"

"Am I?"

She gave him a long look of some sweetness, and he seemed stricken.

"Am I always?" she went on.

"Yes" he said.

"But I was only a child, then, the time you were speaking of."

"Yes!"

"And you found me so, even at that age?"

"You were to me, Ann."

"Then swear!"

He gave a heavy sigh. "Oh yes!" he affirmed.

"I'm beginning to like this better now" she announced, and gave the man almost a warm smile.

"Oh Ann, I've been so distressed about it all!" he at once pleaded.

"About what, dear heaven?"

"Leaving you, like I did, with Charles Addinsell, of course."

"Well I must say I do think you might have rung up, after, to find how I was!"

"But, good gracious, nothing happened, surely?"

"I don't know what you mean" and she began staring round the restaurant once more. "Still, you would have been polite if you had."

"I most humbly apologise, Ann."

At which she gave Mr Middleton a true, warm smile.

"Then you're forgiven. There!" she said. "Arthur, tell me more about him."

"Charles?"

"Of course."

"Well, darling, it's hard to know where to start."

"Have you known him long?" she prompted.

"For years and years. Charles is a strange fellow." Again Mr Middleton fell silent.

"He said you'd been at school together?"

"Yes indeed. He was an odd sort of chap, even then."

"In what way, Arthur?" Miss Paynton appeared quite intrigued.

"Well I don't want to sound arch, and it's really very difficult to explain . . . " he began once more, at which she let out a screech of amused interruption.

"You're too shy to admit that when he was at school Charles used to look at other boys, like Terry does? Is that so?"

"Good God, no!" Mr Middleton protested. "No, as a matter of fact, he always did on older women, very much older."

"But that's only natural, surely? Couldn't you, then?"

"Now why should you think I'm that type?"

"I imagined all little boys were seduced by their aunties' old girl friends."

"Really Ann!" Arthur Middleton sounded quite shocked.

"Then how did it happen to you? Arthur; don't be so puritanical, now please!"

"Well, I'll save that up for another place, and a different time of day, if you like."

She gave him a look and let out rather a deep laugh.

"All right! So go on, do, about Charles" she commanded.

"You may be right when you say all boys start with an older woman" he began once more. "I wouldn't know and I can't admit I myself did, but we aren't talking about me now, we're discussing Charles. And, in his case, it was that." Mr Middleton came to a full stop again.

"Oh, who was it, then? You must tell the name, Arthur."

"I don't know."

"Are you just being horridly discreet?"

"Honest, I'm not."

"Then how can you be sure about him?"

"I wouldn't be certain if she'd told me herself, whoever she may have been." He sighed. "People lie like troopers over these things" he added. "Amazing to think she's probably a grandmother, if she's still alive today. Well, Ann, you can just take it from me, in his case, he always did prefer very much older women."

"You're talking about the first time he fell in love? All right, then. Perhaps."

"I don't know so much about the love part" Arthur said, with a smile.

"Don't laugh!" she commanded, sharply. "This is serious."

"I'm sorry, Ann. But the odd thing is, it has always been older women with old Charles, ever since."

Miss Paynton snorted, in evident amusement.

"Like me, then!" she announced.

"How on earth?" he demanded.

"I've always doted on older men."

"Oh doting isn't loving, at all, Ann!"

"I couldn't say, of course" the girl rejoined. "But this quite gives me a fellow feeling with Charles if all you tell is true. Yet, you know, I'm afraid, you're wrong."

"How am I?" he asked.

"I just do know, that's all" she announced in a dreamy sort of voice.

"You do, eh?" he demanded, accusingly.

"I can't simply guess what you mean, Arthur!"

"Well, you see, I've been friends with the man all these years, and you haven't, darling."

"Ah, but how well have you watched him?"

"Did he ever tell you of Penelope, Ann?"

"Penelope, his wife?"

"Then he hasn't."

"What about her?" the young lady pleaded.

"I'll leave Charles to speak for himself" Mr Middleton said with firmness. "No, it was just that I was able to help the chap a bit over Penelope. When he comes clean to you with the whole story, as he must in time, he always does, you'll agree it bears out what I say."

"Which doesn't sound very nice, Arthur."

"Oh that tale's all old history, now."

"I'm beginning to wonder how much you two are fast friends" the young lady suggested, with a hint of laughter in her tone.

"You ask him. Very grateful to me, Charles is."

"Of course, you did introduce us. He's got that to thank you for, Arthur dear."

"He certainly has" the man agreed, seemingly without much conviction.

"Oh, Charles may have been like that, once" she went on in a cheerful voice. "But he's not any more, believe you me."

"I've known him a long time, remember."

"We won't argue" Miss Paynton commented. "Now tell me your news. How's Diana?"

"Well, she hasn't been too well the past two weeks."

"I'm sorry."

"Yes. But there's been a distinct improvement. To tell you the truth, she's going up to Scotland tonight to be with Peter a few days. He's caught three fish."

"Good for him! Big ones?"

"The biggest was a fifteen pounder. But, I say, Ann, I'm going to be very lonely the next day or so!"

"I expect so."

"I was wondering whether you'd consider dining with me tomorrow?"

"Not if it's going to be like the last time!"

"Well within the next eighteen hours Diana really will be at her brother's."

"If you are going to be horrid like it, I certainly won't come" the girl told him, and made her eyes large with what looked to be reproof.

"I say, I am sorry, Ann! I meant nothing."

"Perhaps you didn't, at that. All right."

"You will, then?"

"Let me look in my book first, please." She did this. "Oh, I'm so sorry, I can't."

"And not the night after, either?" Mr Middleton pleaded, with a very hurt expression.

"Yes, I could then" she said, quite gay. And more seriously "But, I'm sorry, we'll have to go out somewhere. I shan't dine in your flat."

"Very well" he agreed. A few minutes later they parted. As he walked away he seemed, from his expression, to be quite pleased with himself.

That same evening, as soon as Mr Middleton got back from work, his wife arose from her packing to ask:

"And so have you seen her?"

"Yes."

"You are good, darling! I was afraid I was laying too much onto you. What did she say?"

"Not much."

"Then how could you have put it?"

"Well, I told the girl I had known Charles a long time, ever since school days, in fact. That he was a peculiar fellow, always had been."

"And what did Ann say?" his wife enquired when Arthur came to a full stop.

"She laughed."

"She would" Mrs Middleton commented. "But it's one of the last jokes that little thing will get out of this whole affair, I can promise her that" she said.

"How shall I give you the picture?" her husband complained. "It seemed to me her laugh came from sheer disbelief even, darling. That generation simply prides itself on knowing better than ours, don't they? Look at Peter."

"We mustn't mention him in the same breath" the mother objected. "There are certain standards, after all!"

"Oh, quite. Yes, Ann laughed out loud. So I can't quite tell how far this all sank in."

"It will in time, no fear" his wife announced, and went back to her packing. Mr Middleton sat down on a hard chair.

"And did you make an appointment to meet Ann, once more?" the wife enquired, without looking at her husband.

"Of course not."

"Are you sure, Arthur?"

"Darling, what is this? Are you in one of your moods when you're about to claim second sight again?"

"I might be. Yes."

"Well, Diana, you're wrong, that's all."

"Am I? Because I might only be going to the nearest hotel, you know, instead of Scotland."

"Now really! What are you saying, dear?"

"And don't you forget it!"

"Yes, darling."

"That's better" she said in an approving tone. She dropped a nightgown into her valise, straightened up, came over, and gave him a deep kiss right into his mouth, where he sat on the hard chair.

"Yum – yum" he remarked, as soon as he could.

"I do rather love you" she announced, lowering her bulk onto his knees. "Fancy remembering, and keeping up that word all the way from when we were engaged."

"How could I forget?" he demanded, as she kissed his eyes.

"Now, you're not to laugh at me! Particularly not just when I'm being so heavenly with you."

"I'm not" Mr Middleton protested, in a most virtuous voice.

"Oh, heavens, how I love you, God help me" the wife said. While she kissed his mouth with repeated little kisses, she undid a button on his shirt and slid a hand onto his naked chest.

He moaned.

"And you promise?" she murmured, then kissed him again. "No, don't do that!" She kissed him. "You do promise?" And she went on kissing him. "No, Arthur, I told you, no." She kissed him still. "Oh Arthur!" she whispered, in tones of love.

"Let's go to bed" he said.

"But there's no time, oh darling!"

"Two hours."

"I do love you so" she told him, and let her lovely body be undressed.

The next night Arthur Middleton took Miss Paynton to a restaurant they had never yet visited, where they ate, they danced, they drank, they danced and drank again until he told the girl he was not like her, no longer her age, that he must go home. He asked Ann back for another drink. She neither accepted nor refused the invitation, even when he'd given their driver his address. And, in the taxi, she let him kiss her with abandon.

Once they were in his flat, he asked "What will you have? A gin and lime?"

"Just the one" she replied. And when he'd mixed this, she said "You know, Arthur, you dance divinely, you really do! And I'm sorry to say you've my lipstick round your mouth. You must hurry and wash it off while I repair my damage."

"I will" he answered. "Do you want to go anywhere, Ann?"

"No thanks" she said. As he hurried out, she began to put her face to rights in the mirror above Diana's fireplace.

When the man came back Miss Paynton asked, "Why d'you not wish for me to step out with Charles, Arthur?" As she said this, she settled back into the cushions with a sort of easy confidence.

He hesitated in front of her.

"Now, Ann, I never said that, surely?"

"But you meant it."

"Did I?"

"You know you did. No, sit away over there, Arthur, I want to talk."

"Why?" he asked.

"Because this is important" Miss Paynton went on. "It's my life, after all. I must meet people, you do grant me that?"

"Of course, Ann."

"And if I am to meet them, I can't pick and choose, can I? I mean it's impossible for me to ask gentlemen out, I haven't the money, for one thing. So I go where I'm invited."

"But that doesn't prevent someone, surely, putting in a word of warning?" he objected.

"Yet why? I can't see the good. I don't imagine you think I'm blind to how people are?"

"I never thought so for a moment" Mr Middleton protested in what seemed to be some confusion. "Only that with much more experience . . ."

"And I'm earning mine!" she took him up. "Then you do admit, Arthur, you tried to turn me against Charles?"

"Well yes, I suppose."

"But why? Please never think I mind, I don't. I value your interest in me, Arthur, truly I do! Just tell me. What are your intentions?"

"Pure" Mr Middleton answered, with evident amusement.

"That's not very flattering, is it?" the girl laughed. "No, stay where you are now, be a dear! You tell me this elaborate story against a man you introduce one to, and who has since become a special friend, and you won't explain?"

"Jealousy, Ann" the man replied, with a show of modest candour. She laughed, almost nervously.

"Very soon I shan't believe you, any of the time" she said.

Now he did come over to sit at her side. He took her nearest hand, which she left in his.

"I adore you" he assured the young lady, in a bright voice. "I love you."

"You're sweet" she replied at once, without the note of conviction. "But Arthur, you should realise my main concern must be with marriage?"

"Of course."

"You see, I've been wondering if I'd marry Charles. In case he asked me."

"Yes, Ann."

"Don't pretend to be so glum, then!"

"I'm not!" he groaned.

"Oh dear, I am sorry, have I said the wrong thing again?" she wailed. "But I love your interest, truly I do! Yet won't you understand how difficult it is to be a girl?"

"Yes" he gently said.

"Oh I think I could dote on you if I once allowed myself" she cried out, with plain enthusiasm. "You are so sweet to me, you truly are! What would you advise? If he did propose, I mean."

"Turn the man down, Ann."

"But what on earth for?"

"He's got a child already."

"Why shouldn't he, poor sweet?"

"Well, it must be a complication, after all" Mr Middleton suggested.

"No, I fancy there's something much more wrong with him than this little Joe that I've never yet seen" the girl confessed.

Arthur kissed her hand, which she then hauled away.

"No, listen!" she implored. "If only for a short time longer. This is important."

"I am" Mr Middleton protested.

"Then why is it, Arthur, you don't even wish me to stay happy, enjoy myself?" she asked.

"Surely those two things are quite distinct and separate?"

"How could they be? If anyone is happy she enjoys herself, no one can get away from that!"

"Yet if you are enjoying yourself, you needn't necessarily be happy" he objected.

"Well, I think you're just splitting hairs."

"I'm not, Ann" he assured the girl.

"Then I imagine that must be the difference in our ages."

"What?" he cried out. "D'you honestly mean to sit and tell one there's a difference between happiness at forty and at nineteen."

"From all Charles and you have told, I'm beginning to think so, Arthur."

"And what has he said?"

"Well, you see, poor Charles's had a very unlucky, unfortunate life, with a lot of sickness which turned wrong."

"But you're bracketing me with him, Ann, and I haven't!"

"I don't know, and this is not personal, mind, but I find your generation so sad; no, not sad, that's not the right word. What I mean is, you seem melancholy, all of you."

"Can't say I've ever noticed it in old Charles! I'd have thought he was a bit of a gay dog, myself."

"When he can't bear to marry again because his new wife may die like his first one did!"

"My dear!" Mr Middleton protested.

"And he won't really let himself love his little Joe in case the boy goes the way the mother went!"

"No, Ann!" he protested once more.

"You see, Arthur, I'm beginning to think I've come upon a very different side of Charles."

"Is it his true one?"

"Well, his wife did die in childbirth, didn't she?"

"Yes, poor Penelope."

"And you say he oughtn't to mind still?"

"I've said nothing of the kind, Ann."

"Yet, weren't you trying to tell me it was stupid, if you'd already lost one wife, to fear losing another."

"It's unnatural, that's all."

"You mean it's natural for women to die that way, even now? You're saying they're expendable as regards babies?"

"How d'you intend 'expendable'?" Mr Middleton demanded, with obvious bewilderment.

"I don't know" the young lady wailed. "It's a phrase I use, about myself, with my great friend, Claire, and I'm never sure, quite, just what it means."

He drew away from her.

"Because I could not consider things natural for a moment if anything happened to you while you were having a baby" he said.

"I should hope not, Arthur!"

"Exactly."

"You're just like everyone else" she said, with some apparent bitterness. "You want the best of both worlds. A succession of poor, beautiful women who bear you babies and die of them. Which is intolerably selfish!"

"What makes you think I do?" he appealed.

"Because Charles is afraid for his life to marry a second time, and you aren't" she told Mr Middleton.

"Oh, come here" the husband demanded, putting his nearest arm around her shoulders, and the far one about her lap.

"Arthur!" she said, in the expiring voice she used to close telephone conversations.

He started to kiss the girl all over her face.

"Arthur!" she exclaimed in the same tone. She put her left hand into his right, on her lap, and laced the fingers into his. Apart from that, she let him kiss her, freely.

He got quite out of breath in the end.

"Oh, let's go next door!" the man murmured, at last.

"No, Arthur" she said, in a different voice.

"D'you mean that?"

"I'm afraid so" Miss Paynton answered, and slewed her mouth away from his.

"How can one tell when girls mean no?" he whispered, kissing the lobe of an ear.

"By believing them, dearest" she told the man. He seemed to credit this, for, after a moment, he drew away and began to fiddle with his tie.

Not so long after, he dropped the young lady home, with a polite ill-humour which she did nothing to dispel.

The same evening Mrs Middleton rang Charles Addinsell on long distance from Scotland.

"Oh Charles" she cried, once he had answered "he's already got four fish!"

"Splendid!" the man replied.

"Charles darling, I must see you" she demanded.

"Where?"

"Oh not up here, of course. I'm coming South."

"So soon?"

"You see, Peter's in the seventh heaven with all his success. I can quite well leave him. And I don't trust Arthur out of my sight another moment. Besides, I want to see you, darling."

"Yes."

"I must say you don't sound so very delighted" she wheedled.

"Haven't been able to sleep at nights for thinking of you" was Mr Addinsell's response, in a voice which carried conviction.

"Oh you shouldn't do that, darling!"

"Can't help myself, Diana" he said.

"Then could the evening after tomorrow suit, for drinks before dinner?"

"Of course!"

"You are kind! I've been thinking of you such a great deal, Charles!"

"Damn this telephone. Wish you were here" he said.

Following which, they spoke of the weather for a few sentences, and she rang off.

When the day came Mrs Middleton went round to Charles' flat at half past six. She kissed him on the cheek but moved her mouth away as he tried to put his lips to hers.

While he was mixing a drink, she asked "Did you really miss me, like you said on the phone?"

"Too true I did."

"I missed you, as well."

"Why, Diana?"

"Well, for one thing, you are the one person in the whole wide world I can confide in about Arthur."

"That's a reason. Why else?"

"Which is my secret" she responded briskly. She accepted the drink he brought over and sat down on the sofa at his side. He at once put an arm around her shoulders.

"No, Charles" she murmured, pushing it off with her free hand.

"Whatever you say" the man agreed.

"Now, Charles, I want to ask you over Arthur" she began. "Has he been out with Ann, d'you think?"

"Don't imagine so."

"Have you?"

"I believe I did run into the girl for a moment."

"So you asked her if she had, Charles?"

"No."

"And when it meant so much to me!"

"She'd never have told me true" Mr Addinsell protested.

"But you could have told from her face, darling!"

"Doubt it."

"Now don't be false-modest, Charles. With all your experience!"

"Well, if she had said something, and I thought her lying, and reported to you she'd done the opposite of what she told me, where would I have been with old Arthur?"

"Then you're his friend, not mine!" she mourned, in a low voice.

"You know that isn't so, Di."

"It looks very much like it. Oh anyway, I told him he could take her out the just once more, to get rid of the girl!"

"As a matter of fact I believe I remember someone did seem to say he'd seen them out together."

"Morning or evening?" she asked, in level tones.

"Wouldn't know, I'm afraid."

"Charles, you're lying to me . . . "

"Now I . . . "

"No, don't interrupt, I can see it in your dear face" she cried. "Oh, how you could! And for him! It was at night, wasn't it?"

"Well . . . "

"Oh the brute" she whispered and began to cry softly, not even bothering with a handkerchief. "And at a time I promised reprisals if he did" she added, almost under her breath. "Oh damn, Charles, I'm going to cry" although a tear was already on her chin. "I feel simply awful! Oh dear, sometimes I almost hate Arthur."

"Whatever you do, don't tell the old chap I told you!"

"Oh no, I won't, I promise. Oh damn. Look, Charles, I'm afraid I shall have to go to the bathroom. There's nothing else . . . "

"Well of course. Sorry about all this." He opened the door. "You know the way?" She did not answer. She was sobbing over her glass as she went.

Mrs Middleton did not come back for ten minutes. In that time the man put down two stiff whiskies.

When she opened the door to rejoin him she thrust her finished drink forward. "Get me another, darling, I need it, and please forgive that little exhibition."

"You look more lovely than ever" he said, to which she replied, but gently "Don't be so absurd, dear Charles!"

He rattled the cocktail shaker.

"Forgive me" she repeated.

"For what?" Mr Addinsell asked.

"Because, you see, I simply must know. Has he gone to bed with Ann again?"

"Even if she'd told me she had, Di, I wouldn't believe a word she said."

"So then she has!"

"How can I tell?" he implored.

"How he could! After eighteen years' married life!!"

"Don't let yourself get upset" Charles pleaded, bringing her drink over. "People do, you know."

"Does that make it any better" Mrs Middleton demanded, not looking at him.

"Nothing ever gets better" he replied. "Not at our age" and he put a hand round her waist, at which she moved just out of reach.

"It'll have to, that's all" she announced, with a sort of resigned conviction in her voice. "I can't go on with my life like this."

"Relax" he told the woman, as he came after her.

"No, really Charles, we mayn't dodge one another round the chairs and tables. Now, just you sit down, over there, and think about me for a while."

"I am" he replied, obeying her.

"Then what ought I to do to him?"

"Take things easy, Diana."

"How can I?"

"Have your own fun, for a change. Be yourself!"

"But myself is just what I am being, at this moment."

"And teach old Arthur a lesson."

"Oh, I think mothers, of grown up boys, who go to bed are pretty squalid, don't you?"

"People do."

"Which is no reason why I should" she calmly objected. "Besides, it's so long now, I really believe I wouldn't know how."

"Then you should let someone remind you."

"You, perhaps?" she asked, with a half smile across the six feet of space which separated them.

He gave a gay laugh.

"I'd like nothing better" he asserted. "What man wouldn't. But I know enough to realise I'm out."

"Why, Charles?"

He got up, as if to come across to her.

"No, go on sitting there. Don't spoil everything just when you're about to fascinate me."

"I only wish I could, Di."

"Tell me, then."

"We've known each other too long."

"Why?"

"Well, I mean," he said, in what appeared to be a perplexed voice. "You're the wife of my oldest friend."

"But you're telling me that ought to make no difference."

"Only it does, sometimes" he explained. "No, all I said was, you should teach old Arthur a lesson."

"Very well, perhaps I ought. But who with?"

"Don't you know anyone?"

"Not in that sort of way, Charles."

"Then how about me, in the end?"

"Yet you've just said we've been friends too long."

"I might be mistaken."

"I don't think one ever is, not on instinct."

"So you won't."

"No Charles."

"Can't say I blame you."

"You're rather sweet" she murmured, only she now wore a distant expression. "Oh, my God, will you just please look at the time. I'll be late for his dinner."

"And this is the man you were going to discipline?" he asked, nodding in the direction of the flat she shared with Arthur.

"Oh well" she laughed, came up and kissed him on the mouth.

"One's still to keep up appearances, after all! Hasn't one?" She laid her cheek against his.

"So it's goodnight?" he softly enquired.

"I'm afraid so, my darling" she said, and left.

That same evening, once their cook had left them alone with the food, Mrs Middleton, white faced and in a voice that trembled, said to her husband,

"So you took her out at night, after all?"

"Ann? I don't know how you found, but I did. Yes."

"Why?"

"Because when I thought it over, my dear, I came to the conclusion your suspicions were rather absurd, if you'll excuse the expression."

"Then nothing's sacred to you, now. Is that it?"

"Oh, Di!"

"You promised so faithfully, you know you did!"

"But a promise dragged out of one when you're in a state . . . "

"Is not binding? Oh, Arthur, you've grown double faced!"

"How?" the man asked.

"You say so when I haven't arrived back in London more than half an hour before I hear you've been around with her on an evening out?"

"Who told you?"

"Your own best friend."

"And who would that be?"

"Only Charles Addinsell."

"Oh, don't please believe a word he says."

"Then you deny it?"

"No."

"Well, in that case, where are we?"

"Where we've always been."

"Don't be so sure, Arthur. You might try me too far."

"And how about our old arrangement?" he asked, with an obvious show of indignation. "When one of us gets invited he or she always has gone, irrespective of what the other may be doing."

"Oh darling, you promised, you know you did!"

"Under duress."

"Under how much?"

"That promise was forced out of me, Diana, when you were so upset."

"But it's only once one is truly miserable that one makes people make promises."

"Oh, my dear, you aren't!"

"What?"

"Miserable."

"Could you be insane, all of a sudden? Of course I am!"

"And why?"

"For the simple reason you take out that little creature, Ann, the instant my back is turned, when you swore on your sacred oath you wouldn't, ever again!"

"It seems to me Charles Addinsell is playing a very curious part in all this."

"Now Arthur, I'll not have you draw red herrings across your tracks."

"The first person you see when you come back to London must be Charles? Before you've even said how d'you do to your husband!"

"Of course!"

"I can't spot any 'of course' in this, Diana."

"Really? But I had to find out what you'd been up to, you'll at least grant me that?"

"To do which you were obliged to go to my best friend?"

"Naturally."

"Then how did you get it out of him? By sitting on his knee, I suppose."

Mrs Middleton laughed. "Almost" she said.

"But that's simply disgusting" the man protested angrily. "And what's more I don't recognise my Diana in any of this!"

"Can't you?" she asked, with great calm. "Oh, perhaps it wasn't so bad as all that, though it wouldn't do you any harm to get your imagination going some time. No, I did worm the story out of him, which is the important thing."

"So you admit, Di, that what he told you was just a story?"

"He said the truth, my dear" Mrs Middleton announced with solemnity. "I could read it on his poor face."

"I'm glad it's poor."

"Charles is to this day a very handsome man, Arthur."

"Unlike me, I imagine."

"He still takes trouble" she told her husband, in a dreamy voice.

"What rot this is!" the man protested uneasily.

"How rot, when you've already confessed?"

"When on earth am I supposed to have done that?"

"Oh not often, I'll agree, Arthur! No, you did just now, when you admitted you'd taken Ann Paynton out."

"But, my dear, it was yourself asked me to."

"Now don't play the innocent, and when I'm so tired with the horrible journey. The sky is my witness you swore you would never invite her out at night, again."

"Oh Lord, what have I done now?" he moaned.

"And, in addition" she went on "I may be forced to do what I warned you I might have to. Reprisals!"

"Now, look here, Di . . . " he pleaded.

"Something with, say, Charles which I could afterwards regret."

"With my best friend?" he burst out. "Why, you'd make me a laughingstock!"

"Oh, I expect you'd quite soon get over that."

"How could I, Di? What d'you want? To torture me, or something?"

She smiled pleasantly. "How I wish I just could" she said.

"Well then, everything's hopeless then, isn't it?" he muttered.

"It might not be, Arthur!"

"How's that?"

"I don't want to make you swear, or promise now, any more, but if you just come over here this minute and say faithfully you won't ever again . . . "

He went to her at once. "Oh darling!" he said, it seemed almost in tears as he kissed her. She kissed the man back briefly. "There, that's enough" she murmured, pushing him off. "Now let me tell you about his last fish. It took all of three quarters of an hour to land . . . "

Mr Middleton did not do any work that night. They went to bed soon after.

Miss Paynton had one of her sessions with Claire Belaine.

"Well, how's everything going, Ann?"

"If you ask me I don't think I'm getting anywhere, my dear. I haven't seen Campbell in weeks."

"Oh him!" Miss Belaine commented, with plain disgust.

"I won't give anyone up, Claire, which has become a principle of mine."

"In case they grow what you call expendable?"

"I forget what I meant by that silly phrase. I was miserable then, when I made it up, but now I'm just plain desperate."

"Why? What's happened?"

"Nothing. Simply nothing! Which is the whole point."

"How much did you expect?"

"Why, to fall in love of course" Miss Paynton protested. "Don't you?"

"But there's lots of time still, surely?"

"Is there, Claire? Can you be honest and say that?"

"You aren't twenty yet."

"I think there must be something the matter with me, you see."

"Why on earth?"

"Because I can't love anyone, and I don't remember a soul I have. Not even once!"

"Everything comes with time."

"No, look. There's even the one who fell in love with me, or so he says, and I believe him, when I was eight and kneeling on a rabbit hutch at home."

"Would he be this Arthur?"

"Yes."

"And you don't love him?"

"No I simply can't" Miss Paynton muttered.

"Then how about Charles?"

"Oh, my dear, a hopeless neurotic."

"But I've heard of people who go mad for love of those."

"There you are, you see, Claire!"

"Well, I only wish I had the chance!"

"Why, d'you want to be introduced to him?"

"Me? Good heavens, no" Miss Belaine protested, in a virtuous sounding voice.

"He's quite nice looking, you know."

"Maybe, Ann. But I don't."

"Have it your own way, darling. Then you do think I'm choosy not to fall in love with the first man I see, even if he's old enough to be my father?"

"Well, I've always been in love, Ann."

"I know! You've told me."

"And I haven't even had to speak to them, thank goodness."

"Oh, you are lucky!" Miss Paynton sighed.

"You see, I never meet anyone" the other girl complained.

"Yet you do all day, in the office."

"I know" Claire wailed. "There must be something wrong with the both of us then, in that case. Only, of course, we're at opposite poles."

"And just what d'you mean, dear?"

"That they ask you out and you can't fall in love with them, while they won't invite me, and I do!"

At which the two girls fell into a fit of giggling. When they'd got over it, they talked of other things, then left.

"People can be so extraordinary" Miss Paynton was saying as she sat to dinner with Charles Addinsell in his flat the same night. "There's a girl I know, rather a friend of mine, who simply falls in love with everyone she sees."

"Better bring her up here some time, then."

"Why, would you like to meet Claire?"

"I was only joking. Shouldn't know what to do with the girl."

Ann laughed. "I'll bet" she commented. "There's just one major snag. She can't talk to the person she falls for."

"I might prefer that."

"Are you serious?"

"No."

They both laughed.

"Isn't it peculiar" Miss Paynton began again. "But they say some odd things about you into the bargain."

"Such as?"

"You won't be cross, or offended?"

"Not me."

"Well, they pretend you only like persons much older than you are."

"Men or women, or both, Ann?" he asked, smiling.

"Well, ladies."

This time Mr Addinsell roared with laughter.

"What absolute bilge and bunkum" he said at last, when he could.

"I don't know so much, Charles."

"You mean to say you believed that?"

"What do we ever really learn about other people?" she reasoned. "Not to trust the way they look, and that's about all." She paused.

"No, go on" he said.

"But don't you see, even if you made the most violent love to me the next moment, which you won't" she went on, although he had not risen from his seat "which you won't because I shan't let you, I'd never know?"

"Couldn't you feel?" he asked.

"Do you trust your feelings then, Charles?"

"Of course."

"And ought I to?"

"Yes."

"Well, if I did, I'd have to admit there's something horribly peculiar about me." She paused.

"Which is?"

She gave a giggle that sounded embarrassed.

"It's only I can't fall in love at all, and never have yet."

"Much better not" he said, in a sombre voice.

"Oh, you can be so discouraging at times" she cried. "Now Charles, just try not to head me away from the experiences my life must have in store. I've got to go on living. Don't even attempt to put me off with all the fearful things that could happen."

"All right. But why do you think it so necessary to fall in love?"

"Well, mayn't that be so?"

"No. If you wanted to marry, you could, and have a baby daughter, then get to love him much later."

"Marry without love" she said, in a shocked voice.

"My wife, who I adored, couldn't make up her mind to marry me, poor dear, so I took her along to see my old grandmother, who was alive then, and she told Penelope it didn't matter who you married in this life, you came to love them in the end."

"Oh, but then she must have been one of those fearful Edwardian parents who never had children except by some other man than their husbands."

"No, she was born in eighteen fifty."

167

"Honest?"

"It's true."

"Well then, Charles, I think that's the most extraordinary thing I've ever heard."

"What's odd about it?"

· "Everything."

"Why? Human nature's much the same from one person to another. So long as you don't expect to be happy, you can get to love anyone. Ours is still a very small proportion of the world that chooses their own wives."

"What a man's point of view!"

"You've got to take life as you find it, Ann."

"Well, I don't find that, anyway."

"How d'you know you won't, in time?"

"I'll take the risk, thank you."

As the meal was over now, he suggested they should have their coffee in the living room. When she had settled in an armchair and he was sitting six feet away, he asked,

"See much of Arthur these days?"

"He's a friend of yours, isn't he?"

"My oldest."

"Then perhaps you'll explain him. I think he's really rather strange."

"In which way?"

"Well, he seems so frightened of and yet so fond, about dear Diana, all at the same time."

"Old Arthur's not the divorcing sort."

"I should hope not" the girl said with some animation. "We weren't discussing anything of the kind, not as far as I'm aware. No, I can't see how love and terror can run together."

"Fear of losing what he has, I suppose."

"I'd only say this to you, Charles, but he doesn't seem to have much, would you think?"

"Well, a home, a wife and child. After all . . . "

"Oh I realise that could be everything" she rather quickly agreed.

"Almost all one should ask of life. But would you say he was still in love with darling Diana?"

"Does he have to be?"

"Then, if he isn't, why does he go on living with her?"

"I suppose he's afraid of something worse" Mr Addinsell suggested.

She laughed.

"I expect I'll understand some time" she said.

"Well I hope you don't learn the hard way, as I had to."

"Now Charles, you're not to go gloomy on me again" the young lady rallied him. "In any case I'm rather cross with Mr Middleton, let me tell you."

"Oh?"

"Yes. I never seem to even see him any more."

"Why's that?"

"Which is what I was hoping you'd be able to explain."

"Perhaps he's had the red light."

"Of course not. Be serious. I don't think people ought to drop you suddenly after taking one up, do you?"

"Diana may have read him the riot act."

"Over me?" Miss Paynton giggled. "Oh I don't think so. As a matter of fact she's been round to Mummy and said it was you was seeing too much of me."

The man seemed astounded.

"I? Diana?" he asked, in what could have been an offended voice. "Who told you?"

"Mummy."

"When was this?"

"A fortnight ago."

"But, Good Lord, I'd hardly known you then!"

"Arthur first introduced us, Charles, three weeks and two days back."

"Diana? I can't believe it!"

"Yes, she did. But you don't appear to be very interested in what Mummy thinks."

"What does she think?"

"She didn't believe, either, after I'd talked to her for quite a bit. But in the course of our conversation she said a curious thing. Oh, heavens, there I go again! I'd sworn to myself I'd never mention this."

"Go. on, I'm like the grave, I don't talk."

"Oh no, I couldn't. Why you'd never speak to me for ages."

"Come on, Ann. You can't avoid telling me, now."

"Well then, if you swear you won't be cross, and since you're practically forcing me on, you see, she said you'd actually been having an affair for months and years with Diana."

"Damn the woman!" he exclaimed, with obvious irritation.

She gathered up her bag, made as if to rise. "If you're speaking of Mummy . . . " she began.

"No, it's Di I meant" he assured the girl. "Who else?"

Miss Paynton settled down again.

"Yes, I thought it was pretty good cheek" she said.

"More than that! She's been outright nasty. And I'd never have expected it of her."

"Wouldn't you, Charles?"

"No. Imagine knowing a woman all these years and then to come on a piece of nastiness like that!"

Miss Paynton kept very quiet.

"Oh, I suppose Diana was just jealous" she said, in a satisfied sort of voice.

"Jealous, what of?" Mr Addinsell demanded. "When nothing's happened to make her jealous?"

"How would she know? Perhaps she just imagined."

"I'm always imagining" he objected violently. "We all are. But that doesn't make me into a snake in the grass!"

"No, of course" Miss Paynton sweetly agreed.

"I'm glad you see it" he said, in a pompous voice.

"All the same I wasn't exactly delighted to have all that told me, Charles."

"I'll bet you weren't. Perfectly rotten for you, I agree."

"Oh, I got over it."

"Jolly decent of you" he responded with sincerity. "What hell everything is!"

"Don't take things too seriously, dear Charles. I'm pretty sure no great harm has been done."

"Oh, I'm all right. It was you I was thinking of."

"You are sweet!"

"And so are you, good heavens! I wish to God, now, we had done something to give them a bit to gossip over."

"Charles" she exclaimed, in an unsurprised voice.

He got up. He came across. He sat on the arm of her chair. He put a hand into her far armpit.

She shrugged. "It tickles" she complained.

He dropped a leg over the side of the chair, began sliding down towards and underneath her.

Miss Paynton let out a small cry. "You're squeezing me up" she said.

"Come, sit on my knee a minute" he demanded, in a small, authoritative voice.

As she settled on his lap, she asked "But aren't I an awful weight?"

"I want to kiss you" he answered, which he did.

"Oh Charles" she said in the expiring breath she used to sign off telephone conversations.

He slid a hand down along her leg, where the skirt ended. She put her free hand to meet it, and laced the fingers into his. Her arm was rigid.

She snapped a kiss at his mouth. "Oh Charles" she repeated once more, into his silence.

"Might as well be hung for a sheep as a lamb" he whispered to the girl.

"No, Charles." She moved away.

"What's the matter with me, then?"

"Why you're perfect, you're sweet" she announced, rather loud, and fetched the mirror out of her bag.

"Oh God" she said, once she had had a look. "No, Charles" when he tried to kiss her again. And within twenty minutes, she'd got out of that flat, and left him behind, as though she'd done Mr Addinsell the greatest imaginable favour. Indeed, from the expression on his face, while he handed her into the taxi for which he'd phoned, it seemed he was fully conscious of his merit. He looked old and sad.

The same night Mrs Middleton was saying to her husband,

"Arthur, I thought I'd ask Ann to tea."

"Who?"

"Ann Paynton."

"What for?"

"And her friend Claire what's-her-name."

Mr Middleton went back to his papers, even hid his face inside the dispatch case.

"Belaine" he faintly said.

"It would be so much easier if you asked them, darling" Diana propounded.

"Oh?" he echoed, in a muffled voice.

"Yes, and then didn't turn up, so I could have both alone for a change."

"But I've never even met Claire."

"That need make no difference. Just get your secretary to ring Ann up as you do first thing in the office every morning and ask her to bring the friend along."

"I know, and what for?" he demanded, showing his face once more, which had a look of panic.

"I just want to be friendly" his wife replied.

"And you don't wish me to be present?"

Diana smiled at him without replying.

"But mightn't that seem rather rude?" he enquired.

"You could be detained at the office, like you so often are."

"What for?"

"Oh I'm sure you can think something up."

"No, darling" the husband wailed, and wore a frown between his eyes "I meant, why d'you want to see them?"

"Only I never see Ann except when Peter's up in London. And I thought of asking her friend because Ann might feel rather strange alone with me."

"How could she?"

"I think she may."

"What are you trying to start now?"

"Nothing, darling" Mrs Middleton assured the man, with a bright smile. "Now hurry up with all that stupid work" she said, and gathered her knitting together. "Then come to bed."

"Yes."

"So you will?"

"I shan't be long."

"No, invite them to tea here, and not turn up, I mean."

"All right."

"There's a wonderful darling" Mrs Middleton said, and kissed him on what looked to be a puzzled forehead, as she left.

"This is Claire, Mrs Middleton" Miss Paynton announced, it seemed rather carelessly. "She just saves my life at least once each day at the Ministry."

"I've heard so much about you" Diana told Miss Belaine as they shook hands. "Ann's been so angelic with Peter always, when he's back in London, that I simply felt we had to meet."

"He's been catching salmon, I hear" the girl said, with a shy smile.

"Yes, up at my brother's in Scotland. Such a relief! I can't tell you how difficult it is for children to get even one, the gillie explained to me. And he's had five already."

"Good for Peter" Ann Paynton commented with an obvious lack of conviction while she accepted a cup on its saucer.

"Will you hold yourself ready for his last night, Ann?"

"Of course. As always."

"And how about you, my dear?" the mother asked Miss Belaine.

"I think I'd love to!"

"Wait a moment and let me explain. Every holidays on his last night we take the boy out, and try to show him a bit of life. You're sure you wouldn't be bored?"

"I'd like to see a bit of life myself" the girl assured her.

"Oh dear, but you must always be going out?"

"I don't."

"Of course in my day there were all those dances."

"You should never believe the half of what Claire says" Miss Paynton interrupted, in a negligent voice. "She sallies off with some young man almost every night."

"Darling, I don't."

"I'm not so sure."

"Well if you will consent to come" Mrs Middleton put in "we must think of a boy for you."

"No no! Please, you shouldn't bother."

"But of course! Oh dear I don't know any. Haven't you someone you'd like to bring along?"

"I could think, of course" Miss Belaine announced with what seemed to be studied modesty. "As a matter of fact" she went on "I hardly know anyone. I don't know the reason, but I do of course, know why, I mean. The thing is I hardly go out at all, I never seem to meet a soul."

"Then that must be set right at once" Mrs Middleton pronounced with firmness. "A lovely creature like you. Oh dear, but of course, for the evening we're supposing, Peter gets so shy with grown up lads just out of school, so many boys his age are like that, and if we brought one along, well I'm afraid Peter would just dry up, and not say a word. So, for this particular evening, my dear, would you say no to an older man, one of my contemporaries, in fact?"

"Why you are sweet and kind. Of course not!"

"Who were you thinking of?" Miss Paynton enquired, as she raised a piece of cake to her mouth.

"Charles Addinsell" Mrs Middleton told the girl, with great calm. "A very dear friend of Arthur's and mine from the old days" she explained to Claire Belaine.

Miss Paynton laid the slice of cake back on her plate, untouched.

"Oh you are kind!" the other young lady exclaimed. "Why should you go to all this trouble over me?"

"I want to do something for darling Ann here; pay her back for all these evenings she's come out with us and Peter."

Miss Paynton's jaw had slightly dropped.

"Oh my dear" Mrs Middleton exclaimed to the girl, with a sweet, blank expression. "I'd quite forgot you knew Charles already. Won't it be very dull for you if we invite him?"

"Not really" Ann almost gasped. "I mean it would be quite all right. That's to say I don't mind who you ask. I so love coming always, you see."

"So sweet" Mrs Middleton commented, in fervent tones. At this point her husband burst into the room with his briefcase.

"Hullo, hullo, hello" he cried, shaking Miss Paynton's hand with both of his.

"Darling you said you'd be late" his wife reproved him.

"Couldn't resist seeing Ann again" he said.

"You don't know Claire, do you?" the young lady asked. He greeted this girl.

"Did the meeting get through quicker than you expected, then?" Mrs Middleton insisted.

"Yes" her husband answered. "And what have you wonderful creatures been up to?"

"Why, we were talking of Peter" Diana told him.

"He hasn't caught still another fish, has he?"

"Not yet. Now here's your tea."

"Ta. Ann, you look lovely."

"Thank you very much" she replied, in a small voice.

"I'd just asked Claire, here, to come out with us on Peter's last night, Arthur."

"Splendid" the man said, heartily.

"Oh darling" Miss Paynton interrupted, in the direction of her friend "don't you think we should be on our way, now?"

Miss Belaine seemed rather disconcerted.

"So early!" Arthur cried, with obvious disappointment.

"Yes, must you go?" his wife murmured, but it was hard to tell if she meant it from the tone of voice she used.

Nevertheless Ann had her own way quite soon, and took the other girl with her when she left.

"Well, the two of them didn't stay long, did they?" Mr Middleton remarked as he came back from showing the young ladies out.

"Your fault for returning so soon" his wife responded, and seemed dissatisfied.

"My dear, I'm sorry" he said. "We got through quicker than I'd expected."

"Sure you didn't just long to see Ann once more?"

"Don't be so absurd, Di please!"

"Well you won't have much time in the end to wait. Peter'll be going back to school, quite soon now."

"I say, since you've invited this Miss Belaine, my dear, we'll have to find a man for her."

"I've settled all that, Arthur. I told them both I'm getting Charles."

"Addinsell? Oh dear, darling, what is this?"

"Nothing."

"But it must be, Di."

"Very well, then. I only thought for a moment that if you couldn't have Ann, it was only fair Charles shouldn't. Miss Belaine, unless I'm very much mistaken, will create almost a diversion where he's concerned."

"Now look!" Mr Middleton vigorously protested. "You've become almost insane when that man is mentioned."

"And I have certain obligations to Paula, even if you don't think so!" his wife added, in a virtuous voice.

"No, why should you do this to me?"

"What am I doing, then?"

"Oh, I know" he agreed. "But won't it be very awkward?" However, after a certain amount of humming and ha-ing on his part, she cut him short to run his bath, and soon afterwards led him to it.

As the two girls walked away, Miss Paynton explained herself.

"Sorry to drag you off, darling, but all that was too sinister for words."

"Why, in what way d'you mean?"

"Then you didn't spot how Diana announced she was determined to ask Charles?"

"No."

"But it was the reason she invited us to tea. She's off her head in love over Charles."

"Oh, come now!"

"She is! And if she can't get him to take her out any more alone, she plans to use you and me as stalking horses."

"Well, why should we mind, Ann?"

"Yet I do, darling. Oh, I could sue that woman for libel if I cared. The things she's been to say about me to my own mother!"

"You never said."

"Didn't I? I expect that must have been because it all became too petty and trivial for words. Just an older woman's jealousy."

"I see. But I should've thought that might be quite formidable."

"My dear Claire, it's like water off a duck's back where I'm concerned! Luckily Mummy has a sense of humour, otherwise I assure you I'd have been away to the lawyers at once. When women get to the age Di is, they're desperate."

"What's so odd in asking me to meet Mr Addinsell?"

"Or d'you think" Miss Paynton mused "she could be having us along to divert suspicion from herself? Poor, downtrodden old

Arthur could have put a word in, at last, and forbidden her to see any more of Charles, except in public."

"I never realised things were as tense as this, Ann."

"But my dear, it's quite fantastic what goes on!"

"You mean they actually go to bed together all the time?"

"At least I know they try to. You wait until the first moment you're alone with either Charles or Arthur."

"Heavens" Miss Belaine exclaimed, in a calm voice.

"Look, Claire darling, I've an idea. Diana must not get away with this. Suppose you pretend to make a pass at Charles?"

"If I did, I couldn't very well in front of her!"

"To please me" Miss Paynton begged. "Look, I could ask him round for a drink before this party for Peter."

"In front of you, then?"

"Oh, I could go out of the room, for a moment. Yes, that might be much better, to get you to meet Charles first, I mean. I don't trust that woman any more than I can see the nose in front of my own face without my mirror, and she may have something up her sleeve when she asks us both to meet the man. No, Claire, look, it's a most wonderful idea to get him to us, before. Think of her face when she learns you've already met."

"But what exactly am I supposed to do?"

"Darling, if you so much as let Charles lay a finger on you I'll claw the heart right out of your pretty chest. Remember you are my special friend, and that he's mine, until I decide what I want with him."

"Of course."

"I warn you he's terribly attractive."

"Well don't make me nervous, Ann. I expect I'll get by."

"And you promise?"

"Oh yes."

"Because I'll think something up. Diana's just a viper, and she simply must not be allowed to get away with this."

Upon which they kissed and parted. And, as Miss Paynton hurried off, Claire Belaine watched her go, with a frown.

After some discussion the two girls had decided to ask Mr Addinsell to a drink in Claire's room.

"Well, well" he said as Annabel introduced him to his hostess.

"It's so nice of you to come, dear Charles" Miss Paynton murmured.

"Decent of you to take pity on me like this" the man gallantly replied, and seemed to pay great attention to Miss Belaine's roundnesses.

"Claire saves my life every day in the office" Ann explained.

"Is that so?"

"Oh I don't. But you see, they're a queer crowd, and Ann and I rather hang together."

"I thought you should meet Claire" Miss Paynton then explained. "Because, I understand we're all going to be asked on a party and I decided we might have a get together first."

"When's this? No one's said anything to me."

"Haven't they, Charles? How remiss of Arthur."

"Is the date fixed, Ann? Might be going somewhere else."

"It's one of these special do's they lay on for Peter the night before he goes back to school. Oh Charles, you shan't cry off! I've had to carry the torch alone for ages."

"Could be my Joe's last evening."

"Then why don't you bring him along, as well?" Claire asked.

"Too young."

"Oh damn, you're not to drop out of this now?" Miss Paynton protested. "Just when, for a certain reason, it's become quite important."

"Heavens, we haven't even given you a drink yet" Claire cried and left the room.

"Don't you think she's sweet?" the other girl whispered.

"I certainly do, Ann."

"Then be very nice to her. She's had a bad time."

Mr Addinsell was just saying he was sorry to hear that when Claire returned with a tray of every imaginable savoury, on toast.

"What's so sad?" she asked, brightly.

"Oh a little thing to do with old Prior" Mr Addinsell said, at once.

"Your father?" the girl enquired of Ann. "And you never told!"

"Oh something's always the matter now with Dads. No darling, it's nothing."

"I'll get the drinks" Claire announced, and left the room again.

"Please leave Dads out, Charles" Ann demanded with spirit, in a low voice.

"Sorry" the man muttered. "Couldn't think of anything else on the spur of the moment."

"He shames us so!" she almost wept.

"Now Ann!"

Upon which Miss Belaine came in once more with a second tray, a bottle of gin, glasses, lime juice, water and ginger ale.

"Sit down, why don't you" the young woman cried. "I must say, Ann, you're not looking very festive! What are you groaning about now?"

"Not over this spread!" Mr Addinsell exclaimed.

"Go on, then. Mix your own drink, why won't you?"

Upon which the man poured himself out a very stiff gin. Into it he put a little water.

Both girls cried out, wouldn't he like something else, orange or Coca-Cola?

"No thanks" he replied. "As it is, now, anyone who didn't know would think I was on the waggon. So Arthur's to ask us all out together, then?"

"He told me he was."

"What did Di say, Ann?"

"Oh she just stood there when he said, Charles. In fact I fancy it may have been her suggestion."

"Then we shall get asked all right" the man announced.

"I fancy we will. Whether we like, or not."

"Don't you want to go, then?" he enquired.

"I love being taken out, I live for it" Miss Paynton explained. "Only I don't know, but I somehow feel Diana is up to something."

"She almost always is" Mr Addinsell agreed.

"Oh, d'you realise, I'm so glad you've admitted that, Charles. There are times she genuinely frightens one."

"Don't get me wrong" he warned. "I suppose she might be my oldest friend."

"Well, what's wrong with that, after all, Charles?"

"Nothing."

"No, with what I just said?"

"I was only being loyal, I suppose. Diana's all right. Known her years."

"She may be for you, but if you happen to be a girl . . . "

"Very well then, how's she behaved now?" Mr Addinsell wanted to be told.

"Look. She had Claire and me to tea. She'd never even set eyes on Claire before. And she goes out of her way to invite her out, on this end of the holidays party, when Claire has never been asked previously."

"I don't see, quite, why Mrs Middleton shouldn't" the girl objected.

"Di may have wanted to make the numbers even, you for Peter, with me for Claire." He smiled at the young lady.

"Why not?" Miss Belaine assented.

"Because, my darling, I still don't know if I should bring you in on this extraordinary imbroglio" Ann answered promptly. "After all, I still have some responsibility towards yourself, you must admit."

"I might be able to look after myself, Ann."

"Yes, don't make old Arthur and his wife into ogres" Mr Addinsell agreed.

"I still can't see why she's inviting us all" the young lady insisted.

Charles coughed. "Aren't you making rather a mountain out of a molehill?" he asked.

"I suppose I might be" Miss Paynton agreed. "Oh dear, I must leave you two for a minute. Where is it, Claire, on your landing?"

"Yes, darling, and remember not to try and lock the door. It inclines to get stuck, and you'll never get out again."

Once Ann was gone, Mr Addinsell turned to Claire.

"Doing anything tonight?"

"No, I don't think so."

"Then how about a spot of dinner with me?"

"But what of Ann?"

"I rather wanted to have a word with you about her, as a matter of fact. She's an old friend of mine, Ann is, and to tell you the truth I'm a bit worried."

"Oh, I wouldn't know anything on that!"

"I wanted to ask your advice" the man explained. "You'd arranged to go out this evening?"

"Not exactly."

"In that case, come along, why don't you?"

"But how?"

"Look, I'll leave, and after a decent interval, I'll ring up and say where you're to come."

"Will it be all right?" Miss Belaine wondered aloud.

"Well, why on earth not?"

"I might" she conceded with a show of reluctance, and then Miss Paynton came into the room.

"Well, my dears" she cried. "Why so glum? What have you two been up to?"

"Talking about you" he said.

"Oh no, but how sweet!" Ann cried. "You shouldn't."

Then, for a time, they went on with indifferent subjects until, despite their joint protests, he made his way off.

"That's that" Miss Paynton said to Claire, when they heard the front door shut. "Mummy's out, so I said I'd find myself a meal somewhere. How about you?"

"Darling I'd love it, but I can't. They've changed the date of my club, and tonight's the night, this week."

"Oh well." Miss Paynton yawned. "So what did you think of him, darling?"

"Definitely attractive."

"So do I. Now I shall have to get going."

They kissed, and Ann left.

That same evening, Addinsell greeted Miss Belaine at the bar of the very restaurant in which Middleton used to give Miss Paynton lunch.

"Well, well" he said. "Nice of you."

"It's sweeter of you to ask me" she replied.

"This is the place old Arthur brings Ann."

"Does he?"

"Didn't you know?"

The girl laughed. "Perhaps" she said. "Is that why you think it suitable for me?"

"Not in the least. I come here because I consider the cooking's best."

"Goody!" Miss Belaine exclaimed. "Although I must watch my figure."

"What on earth for?"

"Fat."

"Good Lord, you aren't."

"Thanks" she said. "But you see, if I didn't pay attention I might be, even more so."

"Never in the wide world!"

"D'you bring Ann here?"

"Now why should you ask?" he demanded.

"I suppose I'm curious."

"May have done."

"Oh, you are discreet!" she remarked, as she sipped her drink.

"Like the grave, Claire."

"Heavens, you do sound sinister!"

"It's not that" he protested. "But it's no great shakes, for you, to be seen here with me."

"Why d'you say this?"

"Call me Charles, do" he said. "Well, you can't much enjoy yourself with a man old enough to be your father. You surely feel you must be polite to him all the time, like you're being now."

"Am I? Then how ought I to behave?"

"Laugh a bit."

"I have. After which you suddenly went serious on me."

"Here, I'm sorry, I do apologise. I didn't mean anything, you know."

"No more did I. There."

"You ever met Diana Middleton?"

"Only the once."

"What did you think?"

"Me? Why, I thought she was sweet."

"I suppose I've known that woman all my life; since I was grown up, of course" the man said.

"Lucky for you!"

"You think so. I don't know. Anyway it's very decent on your part to consent to come out with me."

"Why on earth?"

"Well, isn't it?"

"When I have to go without if I want to buy anything for myself!"

"How d'you mean?" the man demanded.

"Consider for a moment" Claire begged him. "I have the room to pay for. I only earn a few measly pounds a week. It's simply heaven to be asked out to a real, genuine meal."

"Is it?"

"Well, wouldn't it be?"

"I suppose. Yet, believe me, I'm still very grateful."

"Then we both are, one to the other. Which is a reasonable basis to be on."

"Yet you say you actually don't get enough to eat?" Mr Addinsell declaimed.

"Up to a point" she admitted.

"Better order yourself a pretty decent dinner tonight, in that case" he said.

She laughed. "I will!"

"But can't you go round to your parents when you're short of a square meal?"

"They're dead."

"I say, I am sorry! What time did that happen?"

"When I was twelve."

"It's a terrible object lesson, having a father and mother."

"I've never thought so" the girl complained.

"When they die."

"I hadn't seen it like that before."

"Simply rotten on my little boy when his mother left him!"

"You mean she went so far as to run away?"

"No. She died. As yours did."

"Oh I do apologise. Truly!"

"Quite all right" he conceded. "Then who brought you up?"

"My aunt."

"And you don't care for her?"

"If I were you I'd marry again to save your son going through what I did if something should happen to you."

"I'd never seen things in that light!" the father exclaimed. "You mean it might be selfish not to?"

"Yes. Judging by my experience."

"Good Lord. You don't know how interesting all this is to me."

"Of course I may have been just plumb unlucky" the girl explained. "I was a most tiresome, boring child, I shouldn't wonder."

"I'll bet you weren't!"

"But yes, Charles dear."

"You mean you can't go back to your aunt at any price, even for a square meal?"

"Of course I can!"

"Sorry, have I said the wrong thing again?"

"No, no" she cried. "It was me. I suppose there was something in the way you put it."

"I'm a clumsy old fool."

"You aren't old or clumsy. I don't like it when you put on these airs, dear Charles! But what d'you suppose I left my aunt for, as soon as I felt I was old enough to get a job, with only a pound or two a week to my name, which Mummy left me."

"Are you saying this relation of yours was actually cruel to you?"

"No, only that I got in her way."

"A child! In your teens. Orphaned! How could you?"

"You see she couldn't have friends to the house."

"My dear Claire, and why on earth not?"

"Men friends, Charles. I was always in the light."

"Oh!!" he said, in a loud voice.

There was a pause.

"I didn't mean to shock you" the girl began again, in an apologetic voice. "But that's how things turned out."

"What a rotten time you must have had" he said, in muted tones. "No, of course, you didn't shock, I've seen a bit of the world. Tell you the truth, the more I do witness things, the less I like 'em, but then I'm a bit of a cynic, I imagine."

"Does that go for the people you meet, Charles?"

"You mean, what I said about not liking persons? No, not for all of them, no."

"Which is something, then" she said, in a satisfied voice.

"And how d'you find most of those you run up against, Claire?"

"But I've already told you, I meet absolutely no one, ever" she wailed.

"I see. And Ann?"

"Oh, she's just a girl friend."

"I understand, Claire. Yes, quite."

"You can't imagine how it can be for me at my age in a big town like this."

"Then you must do me the great pleasure of coming out again some time."

"Oh now" Miss Belaine objected. "I haven't been saying all I have, so as to get you to invite me."

"It would be a privilege" the older man insisted.

Upon which they argued a bit, and eventually she agreed to sally forth with him once more, on Wednesday, the evening after next. After that, when the meal was over, he took her to a club to dance. They had a merry time.

He dropped her back in his car. Claire was quite passionate when she let him kiss her. But she did not ask him up, not on this occasion.

The next day Mrs Middleton rang Charles Addinsell early in the morning.

"You doing much tomorrow night, Charles?"

"What's tomorrow? Wednesday? No, I don't think so. Let me look at my book."

"You see, Arthur's just told me he has to go to some agent's dinner. So inconsiderate to leave it so late, but there! You know what I have to put up with."

"Lord, I'd forgotten, but I'm afraid I can't this time, Di. Here it is, written down" he lied. "I swore I'd take old Edward Dallas to the club."

"What's 'this time' meant to mean?" she demanded disagreeably.

"Why, Wednesday, Diana, that's all."

"I see. Then why don't you put him off?"

"Couldn't do it. The man only comes up to Town once in a blue moon."

"I think I'll ring Barwood and check with Edward myself about this little trip of his."

Mr Addinsell laughed, in a tone of great good humour.

"You may" he replied "but you know how terrified old Ed still is of girls. You won't get the truth out of him."

Diana giggled. "Is he still? After all these years?"

"Most certainly so!"

"And you swear you're not taking out that little creature Annabel?"

"Ann Paynton? Never in the world!"

"Her real name is Annabel, as you'll find if you try long enough. Very well, I suppose I'll have to let you go, this time. Goodbye for now, dear." And Mrs Middleton rang off.

Wednesday night Charles took Claire out. After eating they visited another place to dance, where they drank, they danced, they laughed; and laughed, and danced and drank again until at last she said she must go. He squeezed her wrist. "Wait for me, please" she begged as she disappeared into the cloakroom, and when, afterwards, they stood at the top of the stairs until they got a taxi, each soberly leant his or her weight against the other.

"I love you" Mr Addinsell murmured.

"You don't" she protested, in as low a voice.

"Oh but I do" he said, and she sighed.

As soon as the doorman had a taxi, Charles gave his own address, in an undertone, while she climbed in. He tipped more than he need.

Once they were on their way, he put an arm round her waist and kissed the girl, at length, on the mouth. She was passive. And the moment he withdrew, he said,

"To go back to what you told me about going to bed . . . "

She responded with a "Sssh – " and set her lips on his, so that he might not talk.

As soon as he could, he went on,

"But you know you said Ann did?"

"I'll bet she does with you" the young lady answered.

Charles did not paw Miss Belaine. He kept an arm loose around her waist and occasionally kissed the soft, moist corner of her mouth.

"Never in the world" he protested.

"Aren't you discreet!" She seemed to mock.

"Just truthful, Claire."

The girl laughed. She kissed him. "You're all right" she said.

"How much all right?"

"Just a teeny bit."

He laughed. They had been laughing a lot. "That's something, then" he said, and gave her a long kiss.

Eventually she broke away.

"See here" she exclaimed with calm. "This isn't anywhere near my direction. Where on earth are we going?"

"I owe you an apology, I said the address of my flat" Mr Addinsell told her in a soothing voice. "Fact is, I just couldn't see the last of you, all of a sudden." He kissed her. "You're so extremely sweet." She kissed him back.

"We'll have to see about this" she dreamily announced.

At which moment they drew up outside where he lived. He kissed the girl at great length. The taxi driver looked to his front.

"Come up just for a minute" Mr Addinsell said at last.

"No, Charles darling."

"Not even for a second?"

"I can't, you see."

"Why ever not? When I promise I'll behave."

She gently laughed.

"You know I can't" she said.

"I just don't, Claire."

She laughed and pecked a kiss at the man. "Oh, very well" Miss Belaine agreed. "But only on the condition you won't be cross if it is only an instant."

He kissed her. "I solemnly promise" he affirmed.

Upstairs there was a sofa drawn up before the fire. He mixed the girl a drink, out of which she took one sip.

"Oh no, Charles, mine is too strong."

"Give it to me" he demanded, and watered the thing down.

Then he came to sit beside her, setting his own glass, the contents untasted, on a stool to the right.

"I must kiss you once more" he said.

"Charles" she gently replied, and held her mouth tilted.

Shortly afterwards, when she was half naked, with her eyes closed, Mr Addinsell carried her to bed in the next room.

Two hours later, he ran the girl back in his car to her digs. She still seemed just as wordlessly contented.

The next morning, when she had telephoned her place of work to say she would not be in, Miss Belaine accepted the flowers which he had sent and which arrived about eleven, but, as soon as Mr Addinsell rang her towards a quarter to twelve, she pretended to be someone else on the line, and, when the man had rung off, she phoned Ann at her office.

"Tell them anything" she told her friend "say I'm ill, I leave it to you, but I must see you. Could we meet later in the pub?"

"You seem a bit wrought up, darling. Nothing dreadful, I hope?"

"No, rather the reverse. Only you may be cross with me, Ann!"

"I shall be? Oh, I don't think so."

"I'm not sure I'll be able to tell you, even" and, as she said this, Miss Belaine weakly giggled.

"Can't you now, over the phone? All of a sudden it seems so long to wait, darling."

"No, I couldn't, not possibly!"

"All right then. At half past five, Claire."

Upon which they rang off.

As they settled down to their drinks in the saloon bar that same evening, Claire began,

"Well I've news about Charles."

"I might have known" Miss Paynton said.

"What can you know, Ann?"

"I guessed."

"Is it obvious as that, then?"

"I'm not aware of what passed, of course! But everything was fated from the first, I'm sure."

"D'you think?"

"Oh Claire it's my fault for ever introducing you two. Yet I don't know. D'you sometimes believe that nothing in the whole wide world matters?"

"Oh Ann, but surely simply everything has supreme importance, if it happens."

"I've a feeling that everything is relative."

"Between people?" Miss Belaine exclaimed. "Well of course!"

"No, as to what occurs between people" Miss Paynton said in a doleful voice.

"But how can you evaluate what's happened, Ann, when I haven't even told you?"

"Thanks very much, I don't think I want to know."

"Then you seem very sure it must be on the dingy side, Ann."

"Isn't everything always?"

"Have we nothing to look forward to, at our age, in that case?"

"Just treachery, I suppose."

"But, darling, what makes you talk like this?"

Miss Paynton laughed in a nervous way. "Oh, put it down to the weather" she said.

"That's not good enough, Ann."

"Very well, then what d'you want?"

"Me!" Miss Belaine expostulated. "But I'm asking nothing."

"So aren't you, darling?"

"My dear Ann, what is all this?"

"Oh Claire I was such a fool to act like I did."

A look of great patience came over Miss Belaine's fat features.

"I blame myself entirely. I should never have done it" the Paynton girl went on.

"But do what, dear?"

"For the most despicable of reasons, too! You see I was so dead jealous of Diana."

"Yes?"

Miss Paynton beat a knee with her hand.

"When that horrible Diana asked you for Peter the other evening, I thought . . . I thought she was up to something, – and when is it by the way, in three days' time? I knew you wouldn't mind, so I . . . Anyway, you both went out; oh you had my blessing, up to a point, of course, because it came to me Diana has some plan which I can't possibly know, and it was only fair that you should get to meet him first in case he tried anything. And now you look radiant and I feel miserable."

"I still can't understand what this is, Ann, but I'm sorry, I truly am."

"Oh well, as I was saying, nothing really matters."

"But my dear, why not?"

"Or I suppose it doesn't. I don't say I put much money on Charles, but I did hope he'd turn out a friend."

"He is, Ann."

"I must go. We'll see. Goodbye."

She left without a smile, and had not even finished her drink. Miss Belaine sat on with a small, guilty and contented grin across her face.

That night the telephone rang in Arthur Middleton's flat about nine o'clock, just when he had started work on the contents of the briefcase. His wife answered, as a matter of course.

"It's for you, Arthur, and I'm sorry to say it sounds like that little Ann Paynton, though of course she won't give her name."

Mr Middleton groaned.

"Hullo there" he said into the phone. "No. Yes." Then after a pause "What? When, last night? I can't believe you." After which he had another bout of listening. "And to think I used to call that man my friend" he said at last. "Yes, thanks, this is very bad" he ended, and rang off.

"To think of it" he said to his wife, in a rather excited voice, as he came back from the instrument. "I'm afraid you're not going to like this. There's more about Charles now."

"I dote on him, and nothing you can say will alter that fact" the woman promised.

"Wait till you hear" he told her, almost with satisfaction.

"And why should I believe?" Mrs Middleton demanded. "Because it was Ann, I recognised her hypocrite's voice, didn't I?"

"Ann rang up then, yes."

"The nerve! So what did she pretend, dear?"

"Only, Diana, that Charles has been out with her best friend, Claire Belaine."

"Which must be just an idle, lying tale" his wife announced most indignantly. "Why, he doesn't even know the little thing."

"Ann says she introduced them."

Mrs Middleton gave a stricken cry.

"Oh but" she announced "then this may indeed be serious."

"Darling" her husband reasoned, "I sensed it could provoke you, but hardly . . . "

"There's no loyalty left in the wide world!" she yelled.

He came over. "Now darling, what's upset things?"

Diana put the pink knitting down and closed her eyes.

"So you get Ann back and everything's perfect, then, isn't it?" she said.

He laid a hand on her shoulder. "I don't even begin to understand" he told his wife in a patient tone of voice.

"I did what I had to with the best of all possible intentions" Mrs Middleton began again, shut-eyed still. "It was all for Peter."

"But how, my love?"

"To keep a home together for the darling boy!"

"Now, Di, just you leave Peter right out of this nonsense."

"I couldn't be expected to go on seeing you make such an utter ass of yourself over Ann, surely?"

"So you brought Miss Belaine in?"

"Because of Charles! Aren't I to have my friends too? Oh darling, I'm so truly miserable."

He slid down the arm of her chair until, with a practised movement, she wriggled onto his knee.

"Still, if you are happy, that is all I care" she murmured.

He kissed her closed eyes.

"You of all people have no cause to worry" he said, with great conviction.

"Yes, Arthur, but I must lead my own life after all."

"I always did think Charles a cad" he muttered.

"More than you could be, my dear?"

"Now, Di, what is all this?"

"When I loved you so!"

"And don't you still?"

"Of course."

"So why does what Charles has so wickedly done, affect you in this way, my dear?" Mr Middleton asked.

"Are you then to have everything?" she demanded, and opened her eyes at last, in an accusing stare. "Ann Paynton, as well as Claire Belaine, if needs be, the whole time?"

"But I don't even know the other girl!"

"My dear Arthur, your intentions were very evident when you met her over tea in this very room."

"And what did I do or say to make you think so?"

"It was the way you looked, Arthur."

"What nonsense, Di" he protested vigorously. "You're mad!"

"I'm saner than you know" she said, and shut her eyes once more.

"Now have you been all right in yourself, lately?"

"Thank you, Arthur, I'm fairly well, I suppose."

"I mean you aren't in the middle of your change of life without knowing, are you?"

She opened her eyes very wide, looked away from him, and drew herself apart.

"Arthur" she said, in a low voice "are you insane?"

"I only wondered, my dear."

"Why do you do this to me?" she whispered.

"My dear darling, what am I doing?"

"You know I'm not!"

"Well, you've got to face things, Di. It will happen some day and I thought this may have started, that's all."

"But why, Arthur, is all I ask?"

"Because you're so peculiar about this whole business."

"How peculiar, when I'm naturally upset for you if your young mistress who has been trying to ensnare the one friend I still have, starts him off with another girl? What would you feel if you were me?"

"I admit none of this, but for purposes of argument I see your point" the husband confessed.

"Oh fiddlesticks, Arthur! And I could think of a stronger word."

"I see, dear" this man said, in his driest voice.

"And you're going to blame me for it?" Diana cried, seeming on the verge of tears.

"How could I, my darling?"

"You simply don't know about yourself, any more" she told him.

"Very well, then" he said. "Let's call this whole party off."

"But with Peter down from Scotland tomorrow night!" Mrs Middleton protested.

"Why not when you seem so frantic with each one of our guests?"

"Well, my dear, wouldn't you be?"

"Quite possibly, Di" he replied "if I was in your position."

"Which is?" the wife indignantly demanded.

"Now darling" he said, with a show of caution. "I just said what I did because you seemed fed up with the people you'd invited, perhaps with reason."

"But how could I, when I've written to darling Peter who we're to have!"

"There was no way I could have guessed that, is there?"

"You might."

"How, then?"

"If you truly loved the boy!"

"Now, Diana, I promise you I simply won't have this! We are not to enter into a competition as to who dotes on him most!"

"Oh, doting!" the mother cried, in tones of disgust.

"Whatever you care to call it, I don't mind" Mr Middleton exclaimed. "Can't I love my own son, even?"

"And do you?"

"Now, Di, I'm not excusing a single word of this! Kindly pull yourself together!"

"To call off the party we've told him about, and on his very last night! Oh, Arthur!!"

"I said not a word of the sort, I'm certain."

"Oh Arthur!"

"Did I? Well, all right then, I take it back, that's all. And you can't stop me!"

"When have I ever said I could?" Mrs Middleton murmured.

"You're hounding me, trying to drive me off the face of the

earth!" he cried.

"I don't know what you're speaking of" his wife answered.

"But when all's said and done, how will it be when I go out with you, and those two girls, and with Charles?"

"That must come down to a matter between you and your own low conscience" Mrs Middleton told the man. Shortly after which they went to bed, where they made love apologetically.

Next morning, Arthur Middleton arranged to meet Addinsell at lunch.

"So you went out with this friend of Ann's?" he began as soon as they were settled.

"Yes" Charles replied.

"At night?"

"Yes."

"And you went to bed with her, after?"

"As a matter of fact, I did."

"You didn't!" Mr Middleton accused, in obvious agitation. "You can't have!"

"But of course I got her into there. It was what she was asking for, surely?"

"And yet, Charles, she's only eighteen?"

"Well, they've got this coming to them, sooner rather than later, haven't they?"

"Why her, after all?" Mr Middleton demanded, as though he was at a loss.

"You'd prefer I'd pick on Ann, and not on Claire?"

"Oh I suppose Ann's old history by now to you, Charles!"

"No, and not by want of trying, let me tell you, either."

"So how about Di?" the husband hazarded.

"Now look here, Arthur, you must take a hold on yourself" Mr Addinsell firmly told him. "Try not to go on like this. I'm saying, you'll get ill! There's not a thing to any of it. My own tragedy is, I wish there could be something. And you sit here, and make mountains out of soft molehills!"

"A little girl like Claire!" Mr Middleton groaned.

"She's not little, she's a great big creature" Charles objected.
"Come off it now, Arthur!"

"I wish I could."

"Then you blame me, old man?"

"I? Not the least bit in the world" Middleton said, with evident sincerity. "No, if you want me to put my finger on the spot, I'd say it was taxation."

"By making everything more expensive?"

"Precisely, Charles. They don't get asked out any more."

"Except for the old, old reason?"

Mr Middleton laughed. "How then are they to meet anyone nowadays?" he demanded.

"Arthur, my dear, I dine out on that, and I can't afford to, either. One should be able to put the little things down to expenses."

"Well, Charles, all I can say is, you're hopeless!" Mr Middleton announced in a most genial voice.

"My dear boy, it's me who thinks you are!"

"But look here, I'm still married."

Charles Addinsell winced. "Don't rub in about Penelope" he asked.

"I apologise for that" the husband said, with sincerity, and there was a pause.

"Then you want to call the whole evening party for Peter, off, is that it?"

"No, I don't, at all."

"Come clean, Arthur. You know that's the sole reason you've asked me for lunch."

"I'll admit the idea had crossed my mind. But Di won't hear of it."

"Yes?" Mr Addinsell asked guardedly.

"On account of Peter" Middleton explained. "The boy's liable to dry up if we put him with people his own age."

Charles roared with laughter. "So that's why you're still asking me?"

"Yes" Arthur Middleton admitted, and laughed, in his turn, with a shamefaced air.

"Well then, I'm very glad" Mr Addinsell said, with evident sincerity. "Because, for the life of me, I can't see why this sort of absurd misunderstanding should be allowed to come between two people like us who've, in the past, been through so much together."

"All right Charles, and I'm not trying to rake up old sores, but it's plain you forget what it's like to be married."

"Maybe so" Addinsell said, with an air of distaste.

"You don't hold it against me that I said that?"

"No . . . "

"Or when I told you I'd thought to put you off for Thursday?"

"So Thursday's the evening? Let me look at my book, Arthur."

"No, see here old man, you shan't cry off now, how can you? What would my wife say? She'd think I was at the back of it!"

"All is well, Arthur, I'm free."

"You mean Di hasn't asked you properly, yet? Oh, how careless of her! Honest, I don't know what she does with her time, all day!"

"That's all right. I was invited. Only Diana didn't seem so very sure it was coming off, this party of yours, Arthur."

"Not going to happen!" Mr Middleton cried. "Why Peter would never speak to either of us again! Well no, as a matter of fact, to be entirely truthful, I don't suppose he lays such great store. In a manner of speaking you could say it was mine, and my wife's, show to show him off."

"I only wish I could do the same, but Joe's too young yet" Mr Addinsell said with great sincerity. Shortly afterwards they left, went their separate ways, without anything else of significance having passed.

That same evening Peter arrived home off the train from Scotland. While his mother laughed wildly as she kissed him and Arthur called "well, there you are" the boy, in a shy voice, said,

"Oh hullo."

"And have you got another fish, darling?"

"Well, yes. As a matter of fact I did."

"Wonderful!" his father cried. "Any size?"

"Ten pounds two ounces."

"That makes eleven you caught, then?"

"Don't be so silly, Arthur! If he's had one more, that makes twelve in all. I must write to Dick. He's been too kind! And did you remember to tip the gillie?"

"Angus? Of course. Actually, because I'd brought in really rather a lot I thought I ought to give him a bit more."

"And how much was that?"

"Stop it, Arthur! D'you suppose Dick won't ask the boy again if he doesn't tip properly."

"Yes, my dear, I do."

"In any case, when you talked over the original amount with me, I thought that was much too small."

"Oh, let it pass!" Mr Middleton begged of his wife.

"Who's coming to the party?" the son demanded.

"Well, darling, we've got Ann, of course. I wrote you."

"Oh yes" he said, as if bored.

"And this time" the mother went on "we've asked a friend of hers, Claire Belaine."

"Who's she?"

Mrs Middleton laughed. "You well may ask!" she agreed. "Then I've invited Charles Addinsell, for myself."

"Oh God" the boy commented.

"But didn't you get my letter?"

"Which one?"

"Telling you who we were to have?"

"No."

"Wasn't that the one I told you to post, Arthur?"

"How should I know, my dear?"

"I truly believe it's becoming impossible to call on you for anything, these days!"

"I'm sure I put every single one you told me into the box, Diana."

"You can't have done, dear, if Peter never got it."

"Did you see anyone besides Dick when you were up there?" the father asked his son, perhaps to change the subject.

"Yes, there was a chap from school."

"Oh, what a bore for you!" Mr Middleton sympathised.

"As a matter of fact I rather liked it."

The parents exchanged a glance.

"Who is he? Shall we invite him to stay the next holidays?" his mother demanded.

"Oh God, no! Not that."

"I see, darling."

"What's Ann up to these days?" the boy asked.

"Much the same as usual" Arthur answered.

"Not engaged to be married yet?"

"So far as we know, darling" Diana said, in a most peculiar voice.

"Are you off her too, then?"

"No. Why?"

"You sounded as though you might be."

"Why should I?"

"I never liked the woman" he told his mother.

"Oh but Peter, you know you've always doted on Ann! For

heaven knows how long you've simply insisted she should come out on our last evening of the holidays."

"Not me."

"I sometimes say we go through this rigmarole of the first and last nights for our own and not Peter's benefit" Mr Middleton diffidently suggested.

"Who to?" his wife at once asked.

"Oh I think Charles."

"Have you been seeing him again, Arthur? What for, this time?"

"Well, he's a friend of both of us, isn't he?"

"You never told me!"

"Is there any reason why I should?"

"No, about your taking him out, I mean" she said.

"Who is, after all, this Belaine woman?" Peter wanted to be told.

Both parents began to speak at one and the same time, then each broke into gay laughter.

"She's just a hussy" his mother told the boy at last.

"What's that?"

"Something almost unmentionable, my darling."

"Then why do you choose her as suitable to meet me?" Peter laughingly asked.

"Look, Diana, can't we call the whole thing off" Arthur Middleton demanded.

"And how would we look if we did, at this late date?"

"Not go out at all! On my last night? That would be pretty grim."

"No, of course we're going, darling. Pay no attention to your father. Now tell me more about your fishing. Did you get your last salmon in the Uil pool?"

After Peter had gone to bed, Mr Middleton returned to the charge.

"No, but seriously Di, why should we have this evening which no one is going to enjoy."

"When it's tomorrow night?"

"What's that got to do with things?"

"I certainly hope you're not going to be disagreeable even over this!" his wife told him. "Just kindly indicate to me how we're supposed to put them all off now?"

"We could say he had 'flu."

"Well, Arthur, I for one am not going to lend the boy's name to a low lie."

"There's that, of course" her husband seemed to agree.

"And I should hope so too, Arthur!"

"Yet if Peter doesn't seem to be looking forward to it, as he so obviously isn't?"

"You heard him, only half an hour ago, my dear, say with his own lips it would be pretty grim if we didn't."

"I know but it's borne in upon me we may have asked the wrong people."

"Oh, darling, can one ever do right with children?" Diana declaimed, in a sad voice.

"I agree, Di. This is all a question of numbers, surely?"

"And what d'you mean by that?"

"Simply a matter of how many people come that Peter doesn't want ever to meet."

"Are you sure all this isn't a fear, on your part, of being in the same room as me with certain members of our party, Arthur?"

"You mean I'm capable of anything?"

"Yes."

He laughed, with good humour.

"You may be right at that" he said.

"Darling" she announced "whatever they may say against you, you're in a way a reasonable sort of husband."

"Who does?"

"Oh, not many people!"

"You're telling me you've been at your old game of discussing me again?"

"I can't always talk about the weather."

"Then I think it's disgusting, that's all" he burst out. "There must be a sort of standard of loyalty in married life, when all's said and done."

"Yet you take Charles out, unbeknownst to me?"

"Why shouldn't I?"

"And you discuss with Charles who should and couldn't be asked on a party for your son's last night, without even a word to me before!"

"It just happened that way" Mr Middleton admitted, wanly.

"How could it have?"

"What can you mean by that, Di?"

"Show me how it's possible to go over such a subject, with Charles, without meaning to!"

"Now, look here . . ."

"No" she interrupted in a violent voice "you did that on purpose, Arthur! After all, Charles is my friend!"

"Of course" he agreed, in evident distress. "But, before you came along I'd, in actual practice, known Charles a fair while."

"He's loyal to me" she cried out, on the verge of tears it seemed. "He'd never have allowed you, if you hadn't forced the discussion on him!"

"Oh, do let's call it all off!" her husband begged.

"What, in heaven's name?"

"This party, the people we know like Charles, Miss Belaine if you like, the whole bag of tricks."

"And Ann?"

"I must be left with some of my friends" Mr Middleton objected. "We haven't been married nineteen years just to look across a table at each other each night, you and I."

"Eighteen" his wife corrected him.

"Eighteen or nineteen, how does that make a difference."

"Then you are truly tired of me?" she wailed.

"I do so wish you'd not speak such nonsense" he said, in a flat voice.

"And I could, where I'm concerned, put up with a bit more consideration from you in the expressions you use!"

"But what is it, after all, that you need from me, Di? When all's said and done, I work all day at the office, I come back tired out at night."

"When you aren't taking your girls to luncheon."

"You know we have our arrangement."

"Damn our arrangement!"

"Very well" he said, in his weariest voice. "All this is simply wearing me out! I wouldn't be surprised if I wasn't ill. What say if we just didn't see any of these people any more, even Ann?"

"But that would mean utter defeat, dear."

"Now what's this, Di?"

"All I'm trying to say is" the wife appeared to explain "if we turned our backs on these people, never saw them more, then we'd have failed in our married life. Paula would be able to say she was right."

"What has she said?"

"Nothing to the point, yet, when has she ever?" Mrs Middleton enquired. "But if we did that, she will. I know about these things, and you don't" she insisted. "I know, Arthur!"

"Very well" the husband said, as though exhausted. "So what's the next step?"

"You'll see, my dear old darling" the woman told him, kissing his mouth. "Now come to bed, do, you look so tired" and they went.

The whole party, on the night, settled down to their table in an establishment which had just recently been opened in the West End of London and where, whilst having dinner, you could watch all-in wrestlers, dancing or a floor show, at one and the same time. This was made possible by the fact that supper tables had been placed on a balcony the walls of which were of plate glass. The corridor for service was on the wrestling side of their table but left a good view of that ring in which two men were to pretend to pull each other apart to the sound of a good dance band, for the diners were drenched, through open windows on the other side, with a great rhythm from two bands that played alternately, while the yells, the groans-to-be opposite would be totally unheard through plate glass which did not have one opening. This place was called 'Rome.'

"Oh heavens" Mrs Middleton announced, as she took her seat "but what if I feel giddy?"

"I'm so sorry, my dear, yet I did think we might try something new, just once" her husband answered.

"Over there's where they'll gouge one another's eyes out in precisely twenty minutes" Mr Addinsell informed Peter, nodding at the empty ring.

Meanwhile both Ann and Claire were leaning out of an open window on the dancing side.

"No Charles, or I shall feel quite sick" Diana implored the man, plainly nervous at the sight.

"Now girls" the husband called to those two young women. "Come back to your responsibilities." Grave-faced, Claire and Ann then sat down to table.

"Poor Campbell is here" the first one said.

"I wish I could do all my work in these places" Arthur laughed.

"My dear, if you did, with your health, you'd be dead in three weeks" his wife told him.

"Now look, Di" Mr Addinsell protested. "What's this? I thought we were all out to have a jolly evening."

"You don't know about Arthur, Charles darling!" was her reply.

"Well I must say, there's no call to bring my health into question right now, surely?" the husband countered.

"Campbell has even been very ill, too" Miss Paynton told them, in a doleful voice.

"Would you wonder at it, in this atmosphere!" Mr Middleton demanded.

"The doctors were very worried over him" Miss Belaine volunteered.

"Who was, and why?" Ann sarcastically asked.

"You told me yourself" her one time friend answered.

"Now illness of whatever kind's a serious thing" Charles Addinsell pronounced. "My experience is, don't ever laugh about it. Can always end in the tragic."

When Claire giggled, Miss Paynton followed suit.

Upon which, Peter intervened. "I say" he said "d'you think I could have a shandy?"

"But of course, darling" his mother told him. "Arthur, when will you just begin to look after your guests?"

"You know what the help is like, in these places, my dear" this man replied, and began to click with his fingers.

"Oh God" the son commented.

"What's wrong now?" his father asked.

"Nothing."

"How have you been?" Miss Belaine enquired of Charles.

"Are you all right?" the mother wished her son to tell her.

"We shall never get a waiter!" Arthur wailed.

"Steady the Buffs" Mr Addinsell said. "Di, you'll feel a new woman once you've had a drink."

"Who'll dance?" Miss Paynton demanded.

"When does the wrestling start?" Peter wanted to be told.

"This is a divine tune" Miss Belaine assured Addinsell at the same time.

And Mrs Middleton put her own view forward.

"Why shouldn't we just leave?" she asked.

"Go? But nothing's even begun yet!" her son protested.

"It is his evening, after all" the father said.

"I'd love to dance" Charles told his girl. "Only, let me stoke up with a drink first."

"I'm doing all I can!" Arthur Middleton complained, and waved violently.

"I know you are, old man. Forget it."

Upon which the near miracle occurred, an attendant came to take their order. Better still, he brought the drinks almost at once. Their host thereupon ordered another round, then champagne for all.

As he raised the martini to his lips, Mr Addinsell gave Claire Belaine a long slow wink, to which she replied by wrinkling her fat nose. Mrs Middleton must have become aware of this, for she reached over and drove a thumbnail hard into her husband's wrist.

Possibly he took it as a love token, because he murmured back to his wife two little words,

"My darling!!"

"Better now?" Charles Addinsell asked his girl.

"Of course" she said.

"When you get down to a drink you seem to want to withdraw your funny nose right out of the glass" he went on.

"Now, Charles, don't start being a bore" Claire answered.

"I'm still not sure I feel all right up here, Arthur" Mrs Middleton complained. "It must be what it's like to be parachuted."

"Drink your cocktail up" the husband urged her.

The next lot of cocktails came, with shandy for Peter, and buckets of champagne.

"Better now, I am" Mr Addinsell announced.

"Oh Charles, you are being rude" his girl informed him.

"Arthur, I feel at last as if I were coming back to earth" Mrs Middleton told the husband, already at her second cocktail.

"Splendid, my dear" Arthur said in an enthusiastic voice. "Now, who's going to dance?"

Peter asked "When do the wrestlers start?"

"Shall we?" Addinsell demanded of Claire Belaine, as he drained his second martini down.

"Yes" she answered, getting up.

They went, and the waiter uncorked their bottles in the buckets.

"Just a minute and I expect they'll be coming" Mr Middleton answered his son. "Darling, will you join me on the floor?"

Diana gave him a sweet, loving smile. "Well, I might" she said, and got up.

Thus were Ann and Peter left alone.

"I rather hate this place, don't you?" she asked the boy.

"I don't know yet."

"I suppose it's useless to invite you to dance, Peter?"

"Good Lord, you surely don't mean that, do you?"

"All right" she responded. "It's your evening. Forget what I said."

"Isn't it bad enough to see my parents making a sight of themselves in front of everybody?"

"But Peter, they aren't! They dance too sweetly."

Mr Middleton junior laughed.

"You'll have to one day, you know" Miss Paynton told him.

"I'll wait until I marry, then."

"What for?"

"Well, my father did."

"I thought you were like me" the girl complained. "Still everything my parents aren't."

"You know I'd only make you look a fool, Ann. I've never even had lessons."

"I might just want to see Campbell for a minute. Please Peter!"

"You'll get plenty of chances later on" this boy told the girl, and finished his second shandy.

"Then how about some champagne?" Miss Paynton suggested, looking at her empty glass.

"You can't want to, before it's cold!"

"Now look, Peter. It's me who's going to drink the stuff, isn't it?"

"Oh all right! If you will wish to be different, I'll get a waiter" and the boy turned to look behind him.

"No, you pour."

Which he proceeded to do. Because he had not dried the bottle with a napkin, iced water began to drip on his thighs. She saw this.

"You'll get all wet!" she objected.

He laughed and said "But I quite like that."

"Yes, stuffy in here" she agreed. Then she giggled. "Such a fisherman, you can't do without cold water on your legs?" she asked, in a teasing voice.

"Damn sight better on a river than at one of these places" she was answered.

At that, the tune having ended, the rest of their party returned.

"Champagne, gracious heaven! Arthur, you are doing us proud!" Charles said.

"All in darling Peter's honour" Diana told him with a meaning look.

"And is he not going to be allowed any?" the man went on.

"Now Charles, behave yourself" Mrs Middleton protested looking angrily at Claire.

"Can't stand the stuff, thank you" Peter said.

At this there was one of those short pauses, into which Claire's voice soared.

"Just one of those girls who make her young men take her to the same restaurant each night only to show the waiters how many men she has" she was saying to Charles.

"Oh, how people can change!" Ann moaned to Mr Middleton.

"Who? Me?" he demanded.

"Yes, I expect" she answered. "But I didn't exactly mean you this time." Then Miss Paynton whispered to the man, "No, it's Claire. Why, she's become absolutely revolting!"

"When, in the end, are they going to start?" Peter asked his mother.

"Who, darling?"

"Why, the wrestlers of course."

"In their own good time, I suppose. Like everyone else."

"And what is that supposed to mean?" her son almost disapprovingly rejoined.

"Oh, my dear!" Mrs Middleton answered. "As you go on in life, I fear you'll find people come more and more only to consult their own convenience."

"But if they're paid to appear?" Peter wanted to be reassured.

"Aren't we all, in one way or another, darling, being paid, the whole of the time? Take tonight. Don't we all have an obligation to your father because he is taking us out in this expensive place?"

"I haven't."

"And nor you should" his mother laughed. "But these girls! D'you think they feel it?" Mrs Middleton said this into a clamour of conversation, so that she would probably not be overheard. "D'you suppose anything means anything to them?"

"I don't know what you're talking about" her son told her in a bored voice. "Why don't you ask Father?"

"I will, at that. Darling!" she called across the table to her husband.

"My dear" he almost shouted back. "Ann here's just been telling me the most extraordinary piece of gossip."

"I'm sure" his wife drily said. "Come on then, let's have it."

"You remember Charlie So and So" the man went on delightedly. "Who got rid of Dorothy in order to marry one of Ann's contemporaries? Well, now he's reduced to this . . . " and Mr Middleton retailed aloud some really quite scabrous details of the jealous life this couple led.

Diana beamed with obvious pleasure.

"Aren't some people utter idiots" she cried.

"Charlie'd better look out for his health, then" Mr Addinsell commented.

"Oh Arthur, you are a bore! After all, I told you not to say" Ann grumbled.

"Darling, this is very nice champagne" the wife told her husband.

"But I don't see this story of yours," Claire expostulated to Miss Paynton "I mean, does it get anywhere?"

"Only as far as one wants to, I suppose."

Arthur Middleton laughed exaggeratedly.

"Good for you, Ann" he crowed.

"Now, dear, there's quite enough of that" his wife checked him.

"Can't one ever tell anything private any more" Miss Paynton demanded, smiling.

"Oh I'm beginning to enjoy this!" Diana said, with an enchanted expression. She raised her glass again.

"Wonderful champagne" Mr Addinsell announced, as he followed suit.

"Now, just watch yourself, then! You know how terribly acid it can be for you" Mrs Middleton warned.

"Oh surely" the man complained. "Just once in every so often?"

"I'm threatening you for your own good."

"But, Di, no one can say I drink!"

"Who has?" she replied, taking another gulp.

At which all the lights were lowered, their table was lit by one small yellow cone aimed at them through a hole in the ceiling and below, on one side, the dance hall was turned, by more switches, to a deep, glowing violet. The wrestling arena was dead empty, darkened.

Charles Addinsell asked Diana "Will you waltz?" She rose and the extremely soft expression on her face was lost as, in sailing to her feet, she escaped the faint light which was directed on their table.

"Ann?" Mr Middleton appealed.

So, in no time, Claire and Peter were left alone, which was the moment the waiters chose to serve melon all round.

"You never dance?" Miss Belaine enquired of the boy.

"No, I don't" he rather nervously answered.

"Well, why should you, if you don't want."

"That's exactly what I say."

"Because if I keep to that, not being critical, if you understand me, it means I can do what I wish when I want, and no one can say a word of blame."

"It kills me to dance" Peter said in an indistinct voice.

"Why not" Miss Belaine murmured, as she watched the dancers.

The cornices, the window embrasures had been decorated with what seemed to be rope fixed to the wall. This feature had, of course, disappeared in this new darkness. But then just as Peter was starting on his melon, someone, obviously very late, turned another switch and all this, which had looked like rope, broke into colour from within, a pale rose, which framed everything.

"Oh God" young Mr Middleton exclaimed.

"Would you like some of my champagne?"

He nodded, and drained her glass.

"Let me pour you some more" he suggested.

"All right" Miss Belaine agreed. "There's a clean one on the next-door table and no one will notice your dirty glass in this light, even if somebody comes."

This Peter did, and came back to what was now his goblet several times, when unobserved, later in the evening. This time he managed not to wet himself with iced water.

"Thanks a lot" the girl said. They both watched the dancers circling below. No more was uttered for a time. Then hardly turning her head, she added,

"You might do one thing for me, though, Peter. I fancy I'm in Ann's bad books. If you see her beginning to start in on me try and head her off, will you? You know her so well."

"All right, but why?"

Miss Belaine, however, did not explain, and, soon after this, the music stopped. Diana came back to the table with Charles much noiser than she had been when she was her husband's partner. And Ann was exuberant on Arthur's arm.

"Oh, poor Campbell" she laughed.

"Why, my dear, doesn't he seem to be enjoying himself?" Mrs Middleton indulgently enquired.

The young lady smiled, then sighed.

"It wouldn't be fair to tell" she said, straight at Arthur.

"I enjoyed that dance" Charles Addinsell informed the mother.

"I truly love dancing with you, my dear" she exclaimed, and then to all "Oh, darlings isn't this becoming gay" she cried out, in an exultant voice.

"Certainly is, Di. Haven't had an evening like it, not for ages" Charles responded.

"We'll never have any wrestling" Peter said, in despondent tones.

"My dear boy, of course there will be" his father told him.

"But it's all dark!"

"What then? Don't you know all wrestling audiences stay in the bar till the last minute?"

"Do they?"

"Don't be tiresome, just when we're beginning really to enjoy ourselves."

"Look Peter" Miss Paynton suggested. "You're way ahead of the others with your meal. Why don't you and I go down and see what the form is? I'm not hungry."

"Not to dance."

"I didn't even mean that. Let's find this bar."

"You're not to have a drink there, mind" his mother said.

"Come on, Peter" Ann encouraged him, and they went.

"Like a nursemaid when the kid's crying and takes the sweet little creature behind a tree to wee-wee."

Mrs Middleton laughed. "Now Arthur, don't run the boy down. It's natural he should be disappointed."

"Good champagne, this" Charles announced.

"Good heavens, your glass is empty. Here, fill up. Well, you know, Di, I'm wondering if there is to be any tonight, when all's said and done."

"Oh no, Arthur! After you promised those wrestlers to Peter?"

"But, if they are to show up, they're being a bit slow about it, surely?"

"In any case, he can't have everything. Now should he, Charles?" the mother said, using a suddenly bored voice.

"Got to learn to go without" Mr Addinsell agreed.

"Charles, I believe you're only a great humbug" Claire Belaine announced.

"How's that?"

"Well, I mean, you don't yourself lack for much, do you?"

Mr and Mrs Middleton exchanged a long look.

"Quite right, my dear" Arthur guffawed. "Go for the old hypocrite, why don't you?"

"I say, what's this?" Addinsell cried, in what was possibly mock dismay.

"Now, I can't have my dearest old Charles teased" Diana said with a smile towards her husband. "I just won't stand for it."

"I wish I had the friends you seem to have" Miss Belaine told the man.

"Here's how" Middleton said, raising his glass to the girl.

They each of them drained theirs, which were at once filled again. And then, for no apparent reason, they all burst out laughing.

Giggling now, Mrs Middleton announced,

"And, oh my dears, I'd meant to say something to that young woman tonight!"

"Who, Ann?" her husband protested. "Dearest, be careful. You'll get yourself into dire trouble."

"Yes, I had. But knowing myself as I do, I don't suppose I will."

"Did you?" Miss Belaine asked, with what was plainly intense interest. "Oh good! What was it going to be?"

Mr Addinsell emptied his glass and then, unbidden, refilled it from the nearest bottle.

"I have my little plans at times" Diana told the girl. "And then I so seldom carry them out, which I'm inclined to regret, always!"

Addinsell hiccupped, almost pompously. "Very wise" he said.

"Charles!" Mrs Middleton gaily protested.

"Oh come on, now do!" Claire Belaine encouraged her.

"No, Di. Enough" her husband said. "Why, look who's back so soon" he went on, of Ann and Peter, as they came up to the table.

"There isn't going to be any!" the boy accused them all.

"Any what?" his father demanded.

"Wrestling, of course."

"But it's advertised, Peter."

"I know! What can you do!"

"Oh well" Charles Addinsell commented, and hiccupped once more. "Bad luck, is all I say, bad luck!"

"Now Di, what could I?" her husband asked, in a high voice. "With this in all the papers. And on the bills outside. Wasn't it, Ann?"

"I don't know. Oh, all right!" the girl agreed.

"Now you're not to be tiresome" his mother told the young man. "If there isn't to be any, there just won't be even one wrestler, that's all! When you've been having such a divine time in Scotland after salmon, I do think it's rather hard you should try and spoil our heavenly night out by wishing anyone, even anything, could be at all different."

"I wasn't" the son protested. "Only you said . . . "

"Now Peter!" Mr Middleton warned. "Don't try and put the blame on your mother when it's my fault."

"In what way yours, darling?" his wife wanted to be told.

"There is a bar downstairs, but hardly a soul inside except for one or two old soaks" Miss Paynton interrupted.

"Sounds interesting" Charles announced. "Come and dance, then you show me this place of yours."

The young lady made no move.

"Why not take Claire, dear?" Mrs Middleton put forward with obvious malice. "She's been sitting out up here for ages."

"Come on then, somebody, for heaven's sake" Mr Addinsell demanded, swaying on his feet.

"Oh very well" Claire said. They left.

"He's dead drunk" the boy pronounced.

"Now Peter" Mr Middleton objected. "Watch yourself before you cast adzpersions 'pon my guests!"

"Yes certainly, darling" the wife backed up her husband. "Since you've been out with that gillie you've simply become a bore, that's all!"

"I'm sorry. D'you think I could have some more shandy?"

"Another one?" his father cried. "Won't that be your fourth?"

"No, I've only had two. And I took too much salt with this steak."

"Oh, go on, Arthur" his wife commanded. "Why be so mean, on his last night?"

"I'm not, darling! But we don't want him drunk, do we?"

"Poor Peter" Ann said. "Not much fun for you, at this rate."

"Now, please keep out of this!" Mr Middleton commanded Miss Paynton. "Or rather, come and dance?"

"What!" his wife declaimed. "And leave me here all by myself? My dear" she went on to the girl "I was just going to say something to your little friend she wouldn't forget in a hurry."

"Oh good! What?"

"But Diana . . . " her husband warned.

"Yet, knowing myself as I do, I don't suppose I ever shall" Mrs Middleton continued. Then she paused to drink deeply from her glass. And all, except Peter, did likewise. The mother actually gasped.

"There's been the most extraordinary change in Claire, lately" Miss Paynton told them, in confidential tones. "I don't know if I can describe it, but she's become so ordinary, that's the only word."

"You're telling me!" Mrs Middleton took the girl up, warmly. "Yet, don't you think she always was a little bit, even?"

"It's my fault!" the young lady wailed. "Always has been. One gets so taken in!"

"D'you think Charles is?" Mr Middleton wanted to be told.

"Would you say poor Charles could now be in a condition to tell his head from his toes?" Diana demanded.

At this all, except Peter, drained their glasses. Mr Middleton filled them up again.

"Let live, and let live" he pronounced.

"Charles gets so tired" the wife added.

"But he doesn't work, does he?" this girl asked.

"It's the boy of his" Mr Middleton explained. "Oh sorry, Peter. Of course he's years younger than you! Nine, I believe, in fact."

"Oh God!" his son told him.

Ann Paynton, unseen, reached across and took his hand. But Peter shook her off.

"And Terence Shone?" he asked the girl.

"Now don't mention him!" the young lady cried. "He's out! I'll never once again speak to that baby-in-arms, ever! No offence to you, Peter, of course."

"Yes, quite" Middleton junior answered.

"Oh really, Peter!" his mother objected. "When there isn't anyone at this table wouldn't give their eyes to be your age again."

"I couldn't" Miss Paynton told them.

"Oh well, my dear, you're different" Mrs Middleton admitted, in a grudging voice. "And long may you so be" she added.

Meantime, on the floor below, Claire managed to dance with Charles Addinsell by holding him safe in her arms.

"Comin' back to my place afterwards?" he thickly enquired.

"You're dead tight" she answered.

"Not so much so I can't see that friend of Ann's, the wet poet."

Miss Belaine laughed. "Good for you" she said.

"No, but sheriously, Claire" the man went on. "There's something in this whole evening, you know. Domesticity, what?"

"How on earth d'you mean?"

"Only I might've been wrong when I said I'll never marry again, that'sh all."

The girl giggled. "And what's brought you to this?" she asked.

"Just being with old Arthur, and Di, out on this night out with their Peter. And you" he added.

"Why is it special?"

"Don't sh'you shee it the way I do?" the man demanded. "When I go out with my son we have to trail round the Zoo."

"Yes, but one day he'll be older, Charles."

"I dunno but sometimes you dishappoint me" Mr Addinsell said. "Impersheptive!"

"Now you are being rude, Charles darling" the young lady answered in a glad tone of voice, which seemed to show she did not mind.

"Oh, I feel miserable suddenly" Miss Paynton told Peter upstairs, and his father overheard.

"Why's that, because you mustn't be" the man said.

"Well, Claire and everything."

"You needn't go on apologising for the girl. After all you never invited her tonight."

"You mustn't, my dear, cry over spilt milk" Mrs Middleton put in.

"Will you have some brandy, or something?" the husband asked.

"Oh, it's getting so late. I ought to be on my way home" the girl answered.

"Now Arthur" the wife and mother entreated. "Not another word! I'm sure we've all had quite enough, and I don't want Charles to make any more of a fool of himself than he need."

"How about you, Peter?"

"No thanks."

At this moment the dance music stopped, and the players walked off, except for a drummer. A curtain went up and onto the stage came the identical conjuror Peter had watched on the first night of his holidays.

"Oh God!" he said.

Claire reappeared with Charles Addinsell, holding the man tight by the arm. He did not say a word. While Arthur paid the bill, the girls thanked Mrs Middleton. Ann announced that she thought she wouldn't leave just yet, but sit below with Campbell for a bit. Then, while they awaited Claire and Diana outside the ladies' cloakroom, Charles did speak to Arthur, swaying a little,

"Will it be all right tomorrow, Arthur?"

"Of course" the husband answered.

Soon after which, he left in a taxi with Miss Belaine, and the Middletons rode grumbling home.

The next day they all went on very much the same.

COLEMAN DOWELL SERIES

The Coleman Dowell Series is made possible through a generous contribution by an anonymous donor. This endowed contribution will allow Dalkey Archive Press to publish one book a year in this series.

Born in Kentucky in 1925, Coleman Dowell came to New York in 1950 to work in the theater and television as a playwright and composer/lyricist, but by age forty turned to writing fiction. His works include *One of the Children Is Crying* (1968), *Mrs. October Was Here* (1974), *Island People* (1976), *Too Much Flesh and Jabez* (1977), and *White on Black on White* (1983). After his death in 1985, *The Houses of Children: Collected Stories* was published in 1987, and his memoir about his theatrical years, *A Star-Bright Lie,* was published in 1993.

Since his death, a number of his books have been reissued in the United States, as well as translated for publication in other countries.

DALKEY ARCHIVE PAPERBACKS

Visit our website: www.dalkeyarchive.com

DALKEY ARCHIVE PAPERBACKS

Visit our website: www.dalkeyarchive.com